THE FROGS WARNING

K LAWDIS

The Frogs Warning

Copyright © 2022 by Katina Lawdis

ISBN 978-0-9825511-8-9

Published by Viscus Vir Publishing

CHAPTER ONE

KRIS WAS GROWING up. Like most nine year old kids, he forgot many of the things he did as a toddler. He stopped singing the songs he loved when he was small. Now, his interests had changed. He was always busy after school with homework. On the weekends he liked to play with his cousin Niko, or his friends.

Even though Kris forgot the adventures he dreamed up as a little boy, he still had a brave and courageous heart. But sometimes his daring side could get him into trouble. Once, he decided to collect fire ants. It was a great idea until the day he accidentally cracked their glass case. The ants escaped to his bed. They bit him and his friend during a sleepover. Both boys had painful, stinging bites and spent the night at the emergency room. Then there was the time his volcano experiment exploded. Not only did the walls need to be repainted, but he had red goo in his hair for days.

Even though Kris had many adventures, he never thought they could get any more fantastic than they already were. Well … never thought that until one sticky July day. For on this fated day, he and his cousin Niko decided to go frog hunting. They set their sights on the swampy Charles River. So, this is where our story begins.

"Hey Niko, I hear there are mutant frogs in the river. So much pollution that some have three eyes! I am going to catch one of those genetically scrambled things and study it!" touted Kris.

Niko, who was always up for some action, replied "maybe I could catch one and sell it, I am saving up for a remote control car. You know the one that has sparks shooting from the tail lights."

Kris smirked and shook his head. He was not into cars like Niko. Kris loved nature, science, and any unsolved mystery. "The whole point is to have the frogs for ourselves. But if you insist on charging admission to our friends and family, maybe we can go into business together!" Kris joked.

Both the boys laughed as they rode their bikes in the direction of the river. They peddled along with their metal buckets dangling over the handlebars. Their wooden net handles were pinned under their bottoms. The nets waved wildly in the wind as they raced each other on the bumpy pavement. The sun beat down on them. Sweat rolled down their tanned cheeks.

"In position," yelled Kris as they slammed their heels to the brakes and skidded. The side of a tall, steep hill dotted with gray rock and vibrant green moss was now in full view. Both boys stared onward at the large, quiet body of water glittering peacefully at the base of the rocky knoll.

Niko balanced his muscular body upright on his bike. He jumped off in one easy leap. His strong, thick legs had always been good at that kind of thing. Kris slowly shifted his net and bucket to the ground, moving more deliberately than Niko. Kris, although a week older than his cousin, always had to work twice as hard to be strong and fast.

"There's the rocky edge of the hill. We need to climb it, make our way to the side that faces the water, and bump ourselves down to a position where we can net. Should be easy," Kris said confidently, as if he did this kind of thing for a living.

Both boys left their bikes at the base of the street side slope. They removed their belts and looped them through the bucket handles. They then strapped the nets to their bodies with the make-shift buckle/belt creations. They climbed the forty foot street side hill easily. When they made it to the top, they peered down the hill at the side facing the river. Neither would admit it was awfully steep on the river side. Both boys stood motionless waiting for the other to speak.

Finally, Kris nudged Niko and said "I double dog dare you to beat me to the bottom."

"Age before beauty," Niko countered.

"Oh please. Ladies first," Kris replied.

"You're such a beast-face," Niko said as he laughed.

They both stood nervously for a few more seconds, then Kris took the lead. "I'm going," he said boastfully as he shifted to a sitting position. He gingerly slid himself to a nearby piece of rock that jutted from the hill.

Kris was the lighter of the two boys. Internally, he felt he had an advantage because of that. Niko watched as Kris located another jutted part of rock and moved to the left.

"Quit being such a chick and follow me," Kris yelled as he moved left again.

Niko started to make his way down the mountain. He moved slowly and carefully as he watched Kris get ahead. They moved in diagonal patterns for around ten minutes, nearing the water with each calculated move. Suddenly Kris heard something banging against the rock. Then he felt a sharp thud on his head.

"Sorry about that," Niko yelled. He watched his net collide with Kris and then thunder into the river with an echoing splash.

"Maybe we can fish it back up," Kris called, re-gaining his concentration.

The boys finally made it to a small strip of the hill about two feet from the water. Their sneakers barely fit the space. They had to position their feet sideways to stay secured.

"I don't think we can go any closer," said Niko.

"Yeah. Looks like we need to net from here," said Kris in a disappointed yet determined tone.

"Stinks like your gym socks with only one net," said Niko as he scanned the dark water, searching for a sign of his net.

"OK, you grip the back of my shirt. I am going to see if I can pull our net up," said Kris as he prepared to fish around for the hidden tool.

Niko had a strong grip. With his thick hands he held Kris's shirt. Kris bent over and swirled his net in the water.

"See anything?" said Niko.

"Not yet," Kris replied.

Kris tried again, but this time when he raised his net he triumphantly brought up a tadpole. Both boys looked into the net as the brown tadpole wriggled back and forth.

"Count the eyes," said Kris with an air of authority.

They counted the eyes seriously, and came up with a unanimous two.

"That doesn't mean a thing cousin," said Kris. "Let's try again."

Just as they were about to throw the tadpole in the water, they heard a loud buzz.

"Kill it," said Kris quickly, tones of panic in his voice.

A yellow bee zoomed past their heads. Kris was allergic to bees. He ducked nervously.

"Where did it go?" said Niko. He was ready to catch it in his bare hands and take the sting, which would barely affect him.

"I don't …" started Kris, who ducked again as Niko spotted the bee on his cousin's leg.

"Don't move," said Niko as his eyes zeroed in.

Kris stood still as Niko flicked it off his cousin. He was afraid that a slap to the leg might embed the stinger accidentally. The bee zoomed away.

"That was close," said Kris as he looked around.

"No kidding, bee magnet," said Niko as he returned his gaze to the water. "As you were."

Kris bent over again and placed his net in a new area. "I hit something. Maybe your handle," he said.

"Bring it – ." Suddenly Niko stopped speaking and banged his fist forcefully at his ear.

Kris could now hear the bee. Niko still gripped him tightly with his right hand. In a split second the buzzing grew louder. Kris felt wings in his ear.

Kris's survival instincts kicked in. He dropped the net and batted wildly at his ear. He accidentally hit Niko in the nose. Both boys toppled forward and landed in the water as the bee flew away.

Niko was always a strong swimmer. Although he scraped his leg on something hard, he pushed his way to the surface of the water. He began searching for a piece of rock to grab. He spotted a boulder jutting up from the bottom of the river around fifteen feet away. He swam over and climbed onto it.

Kris loved the water. Despite that, swimming was never a strong point. Niko looked around frantically. He did not see Kris. He began to panic. He thought that Kris may have been bit, and might be having an allergic reaction.

Stay calm, don't panic, Niko told himself as he scanned the water. Despite his quick assessment at the surface, he still did not see his cousin. He caught his breath, slipped off the boulder, and returned to the water to start his search. The water was dark and murky. Opening his eyes underwater was useless. He felt around with his hands, pulling up sticks and slimy leaves.

Kris, in the meantime, was under the water. His leg trapped in what felt like a slimy tangle of branches. He struggled wildly, trying to free his foot. His hands nervously moved to his ankles as he held his breath. He wriggled his leg over and over, thinking that this could not be happening.

Niko dove under the water, bumping what felt like branches. He fought back tears as he searched. His heart was racing as he broke the surface of the water to get another quick gulp of air.

Minutes were passing. Kris felt an urgency to breathe. He needed air. He needed to get to the surface. He fought as hard as he could but his foot wouldn't budge. He again pulled at his ankle. For a split second he thought he felt cold, slimy fingers gluing him into place. He jerked his foot around wildly and bent his body forwards, trying to determine what was holding him.

Too much time was passing, and Kris had to breathe. Suddenly he felt something slicing along his neck. Was that Niko with his knife? Accidentally cutting him instead of the branches?

Kris's fingers moved to his neck as rapidly as they could underwater. He felt them slip into his skin. He was cut for sure. Then he felt the pain again, and again. Unable to clamp his mouth shut any longer, he let out a scream.

Water filled his throat as his hands felt flaps of skin on both sides of his neck. He sucked in the cool dark water.

To his surprise he felt a whoosh of liquid stream through his fingers. He imagined that he was at the center of a pool of blood.

He sucked in more water. He felt the whoosh again. He tilted his head upwards and he opened his eyes. Where was Niko? He looked to the surface of the water. It seemed clearer. He saw the wavy image of the mountain, scurrying fish, and a few tadpoles. It took him a minute to register the fact that he could see this.

Stunned, Kris began to scan his immediate surroundings. About ten feet away from him he saw Niko swimming in a downwards direction. Niko made it to the bottom of the river, then looked from side to side … and strangely did not see him. He watched as Niko returned to the surface.

Kris sucked in more water. He felt his muscles relaxing. In disbelief, he realized he was breathing underwater. A sadness took over. He thought he must be a ghost. Flashes of his mother, his 8th birthday party, his pets, and eating his favorite ice cream flashed through his mind.

Kris cried some tears, then noticed his foot was still stuck. He slowly looked down. His vision grew more precise by the second. He saw that his leg was actually tangled in a fishing line wrapped around a log. He found that strange for a few reasons. Firstly, he could have sworn he felt several slimy branches. Secondly, if he were a ghost, couldn't he float away?

Kris bent over and saw he was close to the bottom of the river. He easily found some broken glass, and used it to cut the line from around his ankle. Once freed, he propelled himself upwards. As he swam up, he could see Niko's wavy body flying up the side of the hill. Clearly Niko was getting help.

Kris felt his head rise from the water. He was about to scream to Niko, when suddenly he was gripped with the feeling that he could not breathe. He gasped and immediately dropped back into the river. He sucked in more water and felt instant relief.

What in the world? Kris thought as he slowly moved to the surface again. This time he poked his head up and gripped his neck, expecting to see blood on his hands. Again, he could not breathe the air. When he examined his fingers he saw they were clean. He ran his fingers around his neck. He felt three smooth slits on each side. And this is when Kris realized he was breathing underwater.

CHAPTER TWO

Several feelings ran through Kris. He was on the one hand scared about his inexplicable transformation. On the other hand, he was amazed that he had the power to breathe underwater. Torn by the mixture of fear and wonder, he told himself to remain calm and stay positive. There had to be a good explanation for what was happening, although he truly could not imagine what that would be.

Kris looked around the once dark river. The water did not seem so inky anymore. He could easily see a group of boxer turtles coasting past him, as well as several silver fish. He was impressed to see so many fallen trees on the bottom of the river. The sandy bottom glittered as he swam, easily navigating rocks and branches.

Kris swam further out. He was gripped by his curiosity. He was intrigued by the underwater world. He momentarily forgot about how serious his situation was. As Kris swam further and further, he came across what looked like an underwater cave. He was eager to see what might be inside. At the entrance of the cave he noticed a pale, large frog. The creature hung silently in the water. As Kris neared him, he noticed that the frog blinked and looked him straight in the eye.

"Are you human?" the frog said in a deep voice.

Kris was in shock … mainly because he just heard a frog speak, and on top of that he could understand him. Kris did not answer. He just stared in confusion.

"I suppose you are not. I have been waiting at this entrance for six years now. I don't think the human is coming," said the big frog.

Kris's mouth opened wide. Some large bubbles streamed up from his face. He suddenly heard his own voice speak. "I am human, if that's what you mean."

Kris was shocked that he could hear his own voice. The sizable frog made his way closer to him. It smiled a wide, surprised smile.

"At last! What took you so long? Blue has been waiting to see you. Please come right this way." The frog turned. It then waved him on with one yellow colored leg.

Kris swam behind this strange creature. They entered the cave. The sides were lit by an array of holes that caught the sunlight high above. Kris noticed a wonderful collection of spoons, hairpins, hooks, coins – human tools which were arranged as decorations in a path. At the end of the path sat a tiny frog. It had yellow eyes, golden markings on its back, and a smile on its face. Kris could not help but smile back.

"Hello," said the enchanting little frog. "I am Blue. Welcome to Defense One."

Kris stared at the frog. He was unsure of what type of frog Blue could be. Although Kris knew a good deal about amphibian species, he had never heard of a frog that looked like Blue, never mind a frog that spoke English. "Thank you, I am Kris. Were you really expecting me?" Kris heard himself say.

"For many years now. You are the human that can breathe underwater without a mask. Why did it take so long?" said the excited little frog.

Kris was confused "I didn't know I could breathe underwater. I do not know what I am doing here, or why this is happening. Is this a dream? Am I hallucinating? Can you help me?" Kris asked in a panicked voice.

The little frog looked puzzled, then said "it is your job to help us. You have been touched by magic. Don't you remember?"

Kris was more confused than ever. The only time he was touched by magic was at Niko's 8th birthday when a magician named Marvelous Marvin bumped into him. Beyond that, he had no idea what the frog was talking about.

"I don't know what you are talking about," Kris said nervously. "Look, I fell into the river and was caught in a fishing line. I think I drowned, and that maybe now I am a ghost. That's all I remember."

"But you will understand, when you can remember. Who is your translator?" the frog asked seriously.

"What's a translator?" asked Kris.

The frog looked surprised, but replied "it's a being or object that has discovered you, opened a door for you, and allowed you to walk among magic. A translator could be anything in the human world. It's clear that you have one. Think!"

Kris felt like he was going insane, like at any moment he would wake up to find himself coming out of a dream.

"I really, really don't know what you are talking about," he said to Blue. "I need help, this can't be real."

"Well, you will understand your translator when you transform into an air breather. The moment you do, look around you. You shall see the being or object that you are connected with. In the meantime, you are here! I do not know when you will transform, but I do know one thing … it's that you must help us."

"I have no idea how to help myself," Kris said quietly as Blue stared at him. "What is it that you think I am supposed to do?"

"Stop the destruction," said Blue seriously. A tear formed in his yellow eye.

"What, like pollution, overfishing?" asked Kris.

"Worse," said Blue. "You must stop the war."

"Ah, Blue. Seriously, the country is not at war," Kris said confidently.

Blue swam up close to Kris's face. The little frog was nearly sitting on the bridge of his nose. "But the world will be," Blue said sternly.

Kris tried to recall recent political events. He should have paid better attention in class, or at least watched more news. He had no idea what the little frog was talking about. He knew that some frogs were endangered, and that humans could declare wars.

"Blue, I am only nine. I am not old enough to do anything about any war. I have not heard about any trouble in the world."

Blue cleared his throat calmly, and spoke again. "It's not what you know human, it's what you dare not too. Frogs have felt the heart of the planet beat for billions of years. We have felt the pain floating in the water as time has elapsed. We can see it underwater. We can hear it on land. We carry that message to our new leader, for his knowledge. It is critical to prepare."

Kris looked puzzled. He had no clue what to think. The frog stopped speaking and waited.

"OK. I will try to help you out, if you tell me exactly what will help. You can count on me. In the meantime, can you help me breathe air again?" asked Kris.

The frog stared onwards and said "night is coming."

With that, Kris felt a sharp pain on one side of his neck. He tasted mud in his throat. Out of instinct, he began swimming out of the cave as fast as he could. He rocketed towards the water's surface.

CHAPTER THREE

SUDDENLY KRIS REALIZED he was holding his breath. He shot upwards. He gasped as his head broke the water. He quickly glanced around the river. He was so far out. The only light came from the stars, which shone above him and indicated that it was night. Kris began to float on his back as he stared at the stars. He was unsure of what direction to try to swim in. He stared up at the sky calmly and thought *so much for the translator showing up.* He smoothly moved his arms and legs, allowing the gentle river to work with his movements. He seemed to float that way for hours.

Before he knew it, the sun was coming up. He was coming close to land. Kris glided into the muddy shore. He figured that he must have jumped a city and landed at the other side of the river. As he walked through a small forest, he realized he was right. He was two towns over. He found a main street. He located a payphone. He immediately made a collect call to his house.

His mother picked up the phone. Her voice was full of worry and fear. When she heard his voice, she started to cry. "Oh honey, are you OK?" she asked between sobs.

Kris told her where he was. She hung up quickly in order to go and get him. When his mother found him, she hugged him with more force than he had ever known. His mother loved him with all her heart. He knew that he was at the center of her world.

His mother was so relieved to see him, that she could only cry tears of joy. She did not speak or question what happened. When she saw the cuts on his neck, she gently caressed his face and said "it will be alright."

Now that Kris was back on land and back in the presence of his mother, he wondered if the underwater experience was some kind of dream. The kind of dream one might have if knocked unconscious. Maybe that was it.

After an hour at the police station, closing the missing child report his mother filed, Kris and his mother got in the car and headed to their house. When Kris got home he showered. His mother cooked his favorite meal. After they ate he received more hugs and kisses. Then his mom finally asked a question.

"Did you get stung honey? Niko told me all about the bee," she started as she stared at the red lines on his neck.

"I must have mom. Although I know it sounds weird, I don't remember it. Maybe I scratched at my neck because of it. Maybe the water countered the allergic reaction. It's kind-of a blur," Kris said.

"Niko said you forgot your EPI pen. Honey you know how important it is to have that with you at all times," she said gently as her eyes welled up with tears.

"I know mom. I'm sorry I forgot it. I'm sorry I worried you so much."

"The most important thing is that you are home, and that you are alright," said his mom as the phone rang.

Quietly his mother got up to answer the call. Kris could hear her in the other room, agreeing to something. When she returned she said "well, someone really wants to see you."

Without a doubt Kris knew it was his cousin. Twenty minutes later the door burst open. Niko barreled through the living room and right into Kris. Niko hugged him forcefully.

"What happened out there? I looked everywhere for you. You disappeared without a trace!" Suddenly Niko noticed the red slash marks on Kris's neck. "Cool!" he said with wide eyes.

"I hardly remember. Niko, I think I got caught in a fishing line wrapped around a log."

"But it was at least fifteen minutes. At least! Even I cannot hold my breath as long as you must have been under. And the police came and everything. You never surfaced. It's a miracle or something!" Niko exclaimed.

Kris could not help but laugh. He also felt happy that his cousin and he shared such a close bond. They were better than most brothers. As the day unwound, Kris and Niko rented their favorite scary movies. They had as many laughs as they could, settling into the comfortable routine they grew up developing.

Their joy at being together was in full force. Niko begged to sleep overnight so they could spend as much of the weekend together as possible. Given everyone's state of relief, both mothers agreed to the sleepover without thinking twice.

CHAPTER FOUR

IT WAS ONLY later in the night, when they were alone in Kris's room under the glow of their flashlights, that Niko started asking questions. "OK cousin, what really happened?"

Kris was unsure of how to respond. "I think I got knocked unconscious," he started.

"I don't think you were ever stung. You were swatting so much that the only thing you hit was me. And that bee jetted off pretty quick. We fell in at the same time, and not far from each other. I looked and looked for you," he said as his voice started to break. Clearly Niko felt like he failed his cousin.

"I know you did, I know. This will sound crazy. I think I was unconscious, and dreaming. I saw you looking for me. I got caught on a fishing line. It took me some time to see it. I used glass at the bottom of the river to cut myself free."

"But no one could hold their breath for so long. It's impossible. And if you resurfaced, why didn't you call out to me? You must have resurfaced," insisted Niko.

"I know it's crazy. Maybe I was unconscious and the dreamy state preserved me or something. Like in that movie where the lady is submerged in freezing water for like thirty minutes, then comes back to life."

"Kris, you know that was freezing water. This was *not* freezing water. And the cuts on your neck, what gives?" pressed Niko.

Kris stared at Niko nervously, then began to speak. "In my unconscious state my neck slit open and made some kind of gills. I remember breathing underwater, using them to breathe. I tried to come up to the surface to tell you, but the air hurt my lungs and I needed to stay under."

Niko looked amazed. He nodded his head as Kris went on.

"So … I started to breathe underwater. I went for a swim around the river. I found this underwater cave. I met a crazy talking frog who told me …"

Suddenly Niko burst out laughing. "OK, whatever happened to you has officially made you nuts. People cannot breathe underwater. And talking frogs? Come on now, do you think I am stupid?"

Kris was relieved that Niko found the story crazy. He breathed a sigh of relief and said "and this is why I think I was knocked unconscious. Because I had this crazy frog dream."

"You have always had a wild imagination. Let's get some sleep," offered Niko as he rolled towards the wall and chuckled again. "Talking frog," he whispered to himself.

Although Kris felt a little stung by Niko's lack of confidence in his story, he knew that what he remembered in his head really did make no sense. Based on that it was possible that if he were in Niko's shoes, he would respond the same exact way.

Kris turned over his memories of the river for what seemed like hours. While he lay awake, Niko lay comfortably snoring. Usually Kris would wake him, or cover his head with a pillow to stop the annoying sounds. Tonight, he was too serious to think of bothering his cousin. With the memory of the river on his mind, Kris finally drifted into sleep.

CHAPTER FIVE

"**M**ORE AND MORE frogs floating in the river, destroyed," said Blue solemnly as he looked to the water's surface. He saw scattered frogs floating lifelessly on the violent current.

"Emperor, there seems to be no end in sight. The human boy doesn't see it. How can he be the one to stop the attack?"

"Be patient Little. He just needs time," said Blue.

Suddenly a sharp red beam cut through the surface of the river. It sliced through turtles, frogs, fish, trees, anything in its path.

"Emperor," cried Little as he darted away from the unforgiving stream of light.

Blue spun in a circle, one webbed foreleg pressed against his right eye. "I've been hit," he yelled.

Little quickly propelled himself towards Blue and hooked his hind-leg across his back, dragging Blue to the safety of the cave.

"No!" screamed Kris as he jumped from his sleep, staring into a room lit by moonlight. He felt his neck. The skin was intact. He looked to his left to see Niko still snoring away, undisturbed. Kris could feel himself sweating. He looked at his glow in the dark watch to see it was 3:00 a.m. Kris felt thirsty. He tiptoed his way to the kitchen. He hoped his scream did not wake his mother.

As Kris switched on the kitchen light he was startled to see his mother. She was getting a glass of water herself. "Are you OK?" his mom asked.

"I am so thirsty," Kris replied as he turned on the sink faucet and filled a glass.

"Let's sit on the couch for a minute," said his mom. She started to move in the direction of the living room. Kris followed his mother and sat beside her. The cool water felt magical on his throat. His mom looked outside their bay window and remarked "do you remember when we used to look for the brightest star and sing Twinkle?"

Kris was silent. He couldn't tell if the memory of wishing on stars was surfacing because his mom brought it up, or if he actually remembered his time as a toddler. His mother loved stars. As a small child she always encouraged him to make a wish on the brightest star in the sky. In fact, she still urged him to wish on the brightest star whenever they were out at night and spied one.

"The galaxy is so big Kris. There is so much to life. Always remember there are no limits, like there is no limit to how much I love you," his mom said.

Kris let his mother's words wash over him. Her creative ways of describing the world, and her love for him, always made him glow inside. Kris realized his thirst was gone. He reached over and hugged his mom. He peered into the night sky and saw the brightest star. He made a wish that they would always have these moments.

After his wish, Kris and his mom returned to their rooms to try and sleep. Kris lay back down in bed, concentrating on the details of the dream that woke him. He wondered why his mind could not let the images of the frogs go. He felt compelled to understand the dream. He did not fall back asleep. Instead he lay still, trying to piece his experience in the cave and the dream together. The thought of Blue's suffering still weighed heavily on his mind. What if the dream contained a message? What if those cuts on his neck did signify a special ability? After all the cuts were real. His mother and cousin saw them.

Kris contemplated the events of the past two days carefully. He reviewed all the details until finally Niko stirred. Even though it was 6:00 a.m. Kris poked Niko and joked "about time princess."

"Why are you up?" said Niko in a half unconscious state.

"Cause I am not a slacker," said Kris as he laughed.

Suddenly Kris's mother called to the kids "anyone hungry?" Clearly, she could not sleep herself.

Niko scrambled to his feet and yelled "breakfast celebration!" Kris knew what he meant. He knew that his mother would be cooking all his favorite foods for at least two weeks. It was her way of showing her son how grateful she was that he was OK. This happened when Kris fell off his bike and got stitches.

"I know," said Kris with a smile.

"Hey, this is bound to be better than stitches. After all, you survived the river!" said Niko as he waved his fingers slowly and magically at Kris with a smile.

The boys headed towards the kitchen. The smell of pancakes filled the air.

"Auntie, I will take the works," said Niko.

"Already done kiddo," said his aunt. Niko's aunt handed him a plate of pancakes topped with M&M's, chocolate kisses, and whipped cream.

"Alright!" said Niko as he dove into his seat. Suddenly Niko felt wide awake despite the early hour.

"And for you sweetheart," started his mom, "I made your favorite!"

Kris looked to his plate. He saw homemade brownies, milk, fresh cuts of apple, water, and a croissant. "You're the best mom!" Kris said as he sat beside Niko and started in on the brownies. As both boys ate, Kris's mom made herself a cup of coffee and sat down at the table.

"OK, I spoke to your mom Niko. She doesn't mind if you stay the day. I am hoping you boys will want to do something different. Last year we were talking about driving to New Hampshire to take a hike, but we never made the time. It's going to be a sunny, warm day … and no better time than the present."

Kris grinned. He always loved the fact that he and his mother shared so many interests. He had wanted to take this hike for a year now.

"Mom, this is awesome!" Kris said as he ate the remains of his croissant even faster.

"I'll go," said Niko, not quite sure what all the excitement was about. Although he was not sure exactly where they were going, he knew that it would involve some kind of an adventure.

"Why don't you two pack all the gear you need while I clean up. We should get on the road as early as we can to beat traffic," Kris's mom said.

"Sure thing mom," said Kris.

CHAPTER SIX

A S THEY DROVE down the mountainous highway that paved the path to New Hampshire, Kris and Niko kept each other entertained. They played I spy, punch buggy, and mad libs games. The drive was three hours, but the time seemed to fly. The plan was to hike around one of the state's waterfalls. Before they knew it, they arrived at their destination. They parked at the base of a waterfall. Niko and Kris stared in awe.

"OK boys, this is the base. Double check your packs for the essentials," said Kris's mom.

"Honey, toilet paper, band-aids, food, nets, camera, Epi pen," Kris called as he sorted through his pack.

"Cookies, water guns, gum," started Niko as he looked into his bag. Everyone started to laugh at Niko's selections. Niko was always sure to bring non-emergency items.

"If you guys want to move ahead, please try not to go too far. I want to make sure we are all in contact at least every thirty minutes," said Kris's mom.

"OK mom," said Kris as he looked up the mountain. "And thanks mom, this is really great," he added as he hugged his mother. Kris and Niko moved to the edge of the waterfall to take a closer look.

"It's freezing," said Niko as he dipped his hand into the water. He quickly pulled his fingers out. He shook them quickly in the air to try and dry them.

Kris scanned the water cautiously, almost waiting for a frog to leap out at him. "Let's climb," he said as he started to cross the bumpy terrain. Niko gave Kris a nod as they began to move up the wooded trail.

Kris and Niko went ahead of Kris's mom. As they climbed the mountain, they made stops here and there to examine rocks, moss formations, and different types of mushrooms. They kept a look-out for small creatures. At times they photographed bugs and caterpillars. They kept their nets handy, just in case. Kris would at times jot notes in a small notebook, making sure he recorded everything important on the climb. An hour into the hike, all three stopped for a drink and snack. After this, they resumed the climb.

"Hey Kris, we have not caught anything yet," said Niko as he scanned the ground for signs of odd creatures.

"Well, I am not so sure that we will. I mean, maybe we are too loud or something. You know, we are scaring things away."

"So then let's stand still and wait for something to come along. Maybe we can net ourselves a salamander or something else," suggested Niko.

Kris raised an eyebrow and shook his head. "How about if you try the statue approach while I keep on going?" he said.

Niko looked slightly annoyed. He waved him on with a smirk. When Kris looked back Niko was silently crouched in the leaves, net ready.

Kris enjoyed the alone time. Being on the mountain helped settle the surreal thoughts of the day before. It also allowed Kris to see nature through the lens he always used. There was nothing magical about the hike, but rather the opposite. The air was filled with simplicity. The woods contained a reliable beauty that helped him find his space in the great wide world. He, like his mother, was a seeker of all things beautiful.

Kris sat quietly on a flat rock. He let the colors of the mountain fill his mind. He closed his eyes. He felt the warmth of his mother as she appeared and sat beside him.

"Did you notice the clouds today?" she said as she placed her hand on his shoulder.

"Yeah mom. They remind me of cotton candy," Kris replied.

His mother smiled. "You are right, they are sugary and pure, incredible every time. Look, that one is shaped like a star," she said as she pointed towards a striking cloud formation.

As they gazed at the sky, pointing out several aspects of the cloud drifts, they heard Niko making his way up the mountain. He had a big grin on his face. He was holding his net carefully as something small and brown seemed to dance inside of it.

"Told you!" he shouted as he drew nearer.

"Niko, what did you catch?" asked his aunt inquisitively.

"A really cool frog! Check out the eyes," Niko replied.

Kris swallowed hard. "Did you say frog?" he asked in disbelief.

"Yep, and he has the coolest eyes!" exclaimed Niko.

Niko thrust the net forward so everyone could see. Inside was a small brown frog. It was desperately trying to gain its footing in the net. When the frog finally sat still, Kris noticed that it had yellow eyes. The eyes seemed to glow like two stars in the night. For a second, Kris felt faint.

"Isn't it awesome!" Niko beamed. "And because this hike is your cool idea Kris, I want to give this to you as a welcome back present."

Kris took a step back. He was afraid that if he got too close to the frog, it might start talking to him.

CHAPTER SEVEN

ON THE DRIVE back to Massachusetts, Kris was quieter than usual. Niko was entirely oblivious to the anxiety the frog in the back seat was causing. Since he had no clue, he spent at least an hour drilling Kris on frog markings, best foods, ideal cage conditions, and the like.

When Kris's mom asked him why he was so quiet, he bluffed a bit and said he was just tired from being up so early. He certainly was tired from the past day, and a mostly sleepless night. But mostly he was drained from a new feeling bubbling up inside him … fear.

When they finally approached the house, Niko bounded out of the car and straight to Kris's room. He went to find a suitable aquarium tank, to build a small forest for the frog. Since Kris had such a big interest in animals and wildlife, he had amassed a variety of aquariums. Niko knew just where they were stored.

After Niko selected a tank, he went to the yard to find some sticks, leaves, and rocks. He also found a small flat dish to hold water. He gently arranged it all in the new home for the frog. When he was finally done, he took the frog from the net and lowered him into the tank. The frog pressed its forelegs and hind legs against the glass, trying to climb the sides. After a while, it hopped around the cage. It seemed to be exploring its new environment.

"What type is this again cousin?" asked Niko with a big grin.

"It's a wood frog. They are not endangered," said Kris. Even though Kris knew the species, he had never seen a wood frog with eyes that practically glowed.

"You read my mind," said Niko happily, since this was his next question. "Well now you have a new pet. It might not have three eyes, or be endangered, but he is still cool!"

Kris tried to fake a smile. His false face must have worked since Niko seemed unphased by his discomfort. Niko just kept talking.

"My mom is coming to get me now, but I wanted to tell you it was good spending the weekend," said Niko as he impulsively hugged Kris.

Kris knew that Niko still felt some guilt about his failure to find him in the river, and that it might take some time for him to recover from that. Suddenly they boys heard a horn in the driveway. Niko quickly scurried from the bedroom and yelled "later auntie," as Kris heard the front door open and shut.

Kris was hesitant to stay in the room with the frog. He quickly headed downstairs to see what his mom was doing. As he walked down the stairs he shouted "hey mom, feel like watching The Empire Strikes Back?"

Kris heard some pots and pans clanging in the kitchen, and then a chipper "you bet handsome. Get it started while I put this chicken in the oven to bake." Kris headed into the living room. He started to get the movie ready.

In between and after dinner, Kris watched Star Wars till his eyes hung heavy with sleep. Finally, he lay down on the couch. His mom put a blanket on him and brushed the hair out of his eyes.

"You feeling OK honey?" she asked.

"Yeah. I just don't feel like moving," Kris said.

"Well, the triple header is done. I want to get some sleep too. Why don't you go on up to bed?" his mom suggested.

"But the couch is so comfortable," Kris said quickly.

His mom smiled and gave him a kiss. She was unruffled by his desire to stay on the couch. "If it gets too cold down here, there is another blanket in the closet," she said.

Suddenly she went to the side table and then returned to the couch. "And here is your flashlight in case you forget where you are if you need to get up."

Kris was relieved that his mom was so flexible. She had always been the type to look beyond convention. As he drifted off to sleep, he was happy to think of school the next day. He loved the simple routine, as well as the units on science and social studies.

With this on his mind, Kris closed his eyes and went to sleep. Suddenly his slumber was broken by light pressure on his nose. He instinctively murmured "come on Niko" in response to it. A few minutes later, the pressure was back. Then he felt something smooth moving across the tip of his nose. He quickly sat up and grabbed his flashlight.

Kris nervously shifted the beam around the room. He was frightened of what he might discover. After five minutes of this he shut the light and lay back down.

"Like a needle in a haystack, huh kid?" he heard.

Kris jumped up, this time letting out a yell. He flicked on the flashlight. He pointed it in the direction of the voice.

"Who's there?" he demanded,

"Over here," said the voice. "Your lap."

Kris pointed the flashlight at his lap. He was shocked to see the wood frog sitting quietly on his pajamas. "But … how …" Kris stammered.

"You of all humans should know," said the frog. "Everyone is talking about the other night at the river. The story has already spread through forty two states! You are famous."

Kris rubbed his eyes and blinked a few times. He was sure he was in some sort of a dream. While he did this, the frog looked up at him patiently, waiting for him to speak.

Finally, Kris began. "I thought I must have hit my head that day in the river. I thought that everything that happened was just a dream."

The wood frog looked like it was smiling. The creature said "yes, human. For you passage to the underwater realms has also been connected to dreams. Don't you remember?"

"I have a pretty decent memory. But lately all my dreams have been about climbing mountains, battling aliens, and creating bikes that could fly," said Kris.

The wood frog stared at Kris. "Your passage to the underwater realm happened many, many years ago."

Kris looked puzzled as the frog continued. "Don't worry human, when the time comes you will remember. In the meantime, there is much work to do. Do you remember what Blue told you?"

"Not really", said Kris, trying to recall the cave. "I think he said I needed to help him."

"It's the underwater realm you need to help. You see, frogs and more are dying every day. Do you know why?"

"Pollution, poor water conditions, right?" said Kris.

"It only seems that way to humans, because humans pollute. The enemy is clever enough to attack in a time when pollution is at an all-time high. Humans go on each day not knowing what is happening in the waters."

"Back up some," said Kris. "If it's not pollution, then what in the world are you talking about?"

"It's what's *not in this world* that I am talking about," said the frog. The creature suddenly had a frightened look on its face. Kris stared at the frog, entirely puzzled. A deep silence filled the room as the frog's bright yellow gaze grew glassy and watery.

"You see human, frogs have been on the planet for centuries. We hold a connection to ancient times. There were other reptiles and amphibians, though they are now extinct."

"Yes, you mean dinosaurs, right? I study this stuff, I know," said Kris proudly.

"Yes, correct. But dinosaurs vanished, right? And do you know how?" asked the frog.

"No, no one knows how. Maybe cockroaches know. They are that old too!" said Kris in a joking manner.

"Yes, cockroaches know. That's a fact," said the frog assuredly.

"Are you saying that you know…" started Kris.

"Yes, why are they extinct, yes," said the wood frog. "You see, one species of frog was present in the late Cretaceous. This frog species survived the events at the KT boundary, which marked the time when the dinosaurs were wiped out. My ancestors, and the ancestors of all modern frogs, evolved during the Jurassic period. This very group of amphibians has inhabited Earth for 190 million years …. surviving the K-T extinction that wiped out the dinosaurs."

"Whoa," said Kris, eyes wide with amazement. "I learned about the K-T extinction from documentaries."

Then Kris, who was a walking encyclopedia on certain facts, proudly explained "during the K-T extinction, pretty much 90% of marine species, about half of the marine genera, and about 15% of marine families went extinct. As for the land animals, about 85% of the species, about 25% of the families, and about half of the genera died out. Larger animals, like those over about 55 pounds, were all wiped out."

The wood frog's mouth seemed to curl up slightly, as the creature added "frog species survived into the Paleocene, with few species becoming extinct."

Kris, fully well knowing this topic, added "the fossil record for frog families and genera is uneven. A survey of three genera of frogs in Montana showed that they were unaffected by the K-T event and survived unchanged. The data show little or no evidence for extinction of amphibian families that bracket the K-T event."

The little frog's gold eyes grew wider. He could see why Kris was special. Not only did he possess instinct, experiences that he could not recall, but he also had immense historical knowledge.

The wood frog said "amphibian survival resulted from the clade's ability to seek shelter in water, or to build burrows in sediments, soil, wood, or beneath rocks. Our stories have been passed from generation to generation. This is the reason we know what happened to the dinosaurs."

"This is amazing. What happened to them?" asked Kris.

Suddenly the little frog hopped on Kris's shoulder. In a flash the creature pressed its webbed foreleg to the side of Kris's cheek. Although the foreleg was tiny and delicate looking, it felt like a bolt of electricity. This sent Kris reeling back in his seat, with the frog glued tight to his face.

Before Kris could scream in pain, he saw a flash of light. He timidly opened his eyes to find he was staring into a barren, smoky land. He heard ferocious roaring, and booming footsteps. A triceratops entered the scene. He heard the voice of the little frog in his ear as he watched.

"Dinosaurs were a threat to the alien world. Their strength and power made them rulers of the earth. The earth was considered a planet that some wanted to battle for," said the frog as Kris's eyes widened.

"You have to be kidding," said Kris. "Here I thought it was a meteor that might have destroyed them."

"I wish I was kidding, and you are not so far off. Aliens used meteors in battle. Meteors are excellent weapons," said the frog.

Kris watched as the scene grew violent. Large meteors burst from the sky. Fire rained down on the large beasts.

"Millions of years ago, life in the solar system was less desirable. Alien life forms targeted earth. They attempted to take it over, but the dinosaurs were ferociously territorial and they fought long and hard. In the end, the dinosaurs lost. The aliens used meteors to ruin their environment. They generated severe weather conditions. You see, the aliens were clever but not strong. They were masterful, but not large. Their only weapons lie in their intelligence to trick, fool, and manipulate. They eventually killed off the dinosaurs. Frogs and birds went into hiding. But frogs and birds witnessed the war."

"This makes no sense. If what you are saying is correct … then aliens, not humans, would have taken over the earth, right?"

"Well, right and not right. You see, there is already a take-over, but it's not large. Aliens have found ways to live side by side with humans. Aliens still rule the solar system. Earth was just one living option up until recently."

"So, this has something to do with the frogs, right?" asked Kris.

"Precisely. The aliens want to take over the rivers, lakes, and oceans. Their goal is to set up underwater bases. It won't be long until they need more of the land. Then human, the threat will be upon you!"

Suddenly the little foreleg detached from Kris's face. Kris found himself staring into the blackness of his living room. Light from a bright star outside lit the space where the small frog sat on the couch. Kris blinked, trying to register all the frog had to say.

"So human, if you can stop the war underwater, you can protect the frogs as well as your land life. The land will be the next threat. You can help us, which will ultimately help you … but it all starts below the surface."

"But I am just a boy," said Kris seriously.

"Did you not understand me when I explained that the aliens were not large, or strong, yet they defeated the dinosaurs!" said the frog in an exasperated tone.

"Yes," replied Kris.

"So that's the point. It takes cleverness, brains, and incredible imagination to stop them human. You have all those things. You have had them ever since you were a small child."

"How do you know any of this?" asked Kris.

"Just because you forgot, or cannot remember the voyages of your childhood dreams, does not mean they did not exist … or that we did not hear of you then," said the wood frog.

Kris was still confused about remembering his past. This was the second time the amphibians brought this up. What exactly could they mean?

"So human, what are you going to do?" asked the wood frog.

CHAPTER EIGHT

KRIS STARED AT the wood frog. He was amazed by the power in his foreleg, and the message he delivered to Kris. Inside, Kris felt a mix of excitement and fear. Excitement on the one hand, after all he spent weeks convincing his mother he knew more than many adults. Now this seemed to be true. Fear, on the other hand, for entering the world of frogs was unfamiliar territory. Kris had no basis to comprehend the world of outer space, or the idea of life on it.

The wood frog stared at Kris. Its yellow eyes were wide with determination. Kris looked at the wood frog and said "I will help."

The wood frog was delighted. It leapt off the couch and high in the air. It hopped quickly from the couch to the T.V., then to the top of Kris's head. Kris gently removed the frog from his head and placed it in his hand.

"Excellent, excellent," said the wood frog. Suddenly the frog let out a series of croaks. The noises made a strange pattern.

"I have alerted the others human. Now it's time," the creature exclaimed.

"Right now? but it's the middle of the night. My mom will freak out. We need to plan," Kris said rapidly.

"No … time for me to go. You will be just fine. You already know where Blue lives. You will also know the signs when they come. It's time, human, for me to give you my power," said the frog.

"I am not sure I understand," said Kris puzzled.

"You will in time," said the frog.

Suddenly Kris's hand grew warm where the frog sat. Within seconds his hand was hot. Kris's eyes widened in alarm.

"Something is happening. Are you OK?" Kris said as he went to place the frog on the couch.

As Kris turned his wrist to deposit the frog on the couch, the frog melted into a gooey pile on his hand. Kris turned his palm upwards. He saw a thick, bright, yellow liquid running across his hand. It ran all the way down his wrist.

He attempted to shake the substance off. It would not budge. Suddenly tears sprung in Kris's eyes. He realized that the little wood frog was gone.

Kris sat in silence. He stared at his hand, watching the yellow color evaporate somehow. He fought back tears. He realized that the little frog was just some kind of messenger … nothing more.

He got up and headed to the bathroom to wash his hand in the sink. He turned on the water and waited for it to heat up. While he waited, he pressed his hand to the mirror. In an instant he felt a stream of electricity running down his arm. He looked at the glass. He was shocked to see that his reflection was no longer present. Instead he was staring into a watery cave, a place he had been before.

Suddenly a voice emerged from the mirror. "Human, I am relieved to hear that you have joined our fight," he heard.

"Blue," Kris gasped, staring ahead in disbelief at the frog he met in the river. "How is this ..."

"It's a gift to you human. The wood frog's powers are now your own. He needed to sacrifice himself in order to empower you. It was the greatest honor in our world. The wood frog was a mighty warrior, and an old one as well. He has passed his magic on to you. Be not afraid of the power you have gained."

Kris stared into the mirror. He was amazed. Blue's message made him feel a bit less sad.

"Human, it will be important for us to meet in real time. We need to discuss the war, and what needs to be done."

"Yes. I need more information," said Kris.

"And you will have it. It will come through seeing me, and through the memories the wood frog planted in you. Come to the river," said Blue.

"OK. how about tomorrow, in the morning? I need to make up an excuse for missing school," replied Kris.

"Just know, time is precious. Come to the cave. Hurry," added Blue.

"OK Blue. I will," said Kris.

The mirror suddenly transformed back to glass. Kris saw himself staring straight on at his own reflection. He watched a bead of sweat trickle down the side of his face.

CHAPTER NINE

THE NEXT MORNING Kris had a plan. He thought the best way to make it to the cave would be to head there during school. The entire town knew of his ordeal at the river. Kris's mom was always one for letting him stay home, so an absence would not be suspicious in light of the timing.

Kris planned to pretend he was heading to school. He would leave, and then round back after his mother left for work. At this point he would use her email account to message his teacher. He would explain that he would be absent, of course signing his mother's name. He would delete the sent mail. His teacher would not question it. His mom would never know ... easy.

The plan went off without a hitch ... at least not an immediate one. All Kris had to do now was get to Niko before the school day was out. He just had to tell Niko to keep quiet. He had plenty of time to do this.

Kris hopped on his bike. He rode as quickly as he could to the Charles River. He felt a rush of excitement as the wind whipped through his hair. Sweat started to bead on his forehead as he neared the knoll. Kris made it to the river in record time. He was about to venture to the water's edge when he heard "are you crazy!"

Kris spun around fast to see Niko riding up behind him. He was panting. He looked bewildered. Niko jumped off his bike and ran to his cousin. "I thought we could go in together today. I went to your house. I saw you leave and go back in, then come back out on the bike. I was watching you, waiting to see what was happening."

Kris looked panicked. He was not sure what he could tell Niko that would not cause his cousin to run off and tell his mom. His mind raced to come up with a reply. All he could think of was the truth.

"Niko … look, I know this is going to sound crazy. The day I fell in the water, I really did find that cave. I really could breathe underwater," said Kris sincerely.

Niko snorted "I think something is wrong with you. You are like a brother to me and …. are you trying to hurt yourself? I mean, are things rough at school? What's really happening?" Tears sprung from Niko's eyes as he spoke. Niko was confused, scared, and worried for his cousin.

"Niko, I will show you, OK? I do not know how else to explain this. You just need to see," said Kris emphatically.

"Kris, there is nothing to see. No one breathes under-water without scuba gear. Come on! You of all the nerds should know this stuff. You sound crazy. I do not know what to do," said Niko in a panicked tone.

"Then come with me and watch this," Kris said calmly, trying to diffuse Niko's fear. Kris boldly headed to the water, with Niko trailing him by inches.

"You are not a strong swimmer Kris. Don't do this, I couldn't find you last time, I … " Niko started as Kris walked to a rocky offshoot.

"OK, here's the plan. I am going to jump in and see if whatever happened to me that day will happen again. You can dog paddle right beside me. Cool?" said Kris.

Kris jumped in the water. A flash of doubt crossed his mind as he wondered how to recreate the conditions that made him change to a water breather in the first place. Niko dove in strongly right after him. He treaded water easily as he watched Kris bob back up.

"You are not a fish Kris. You look the same. I think this proves my point," said Niko in a frustrated tone.

"Hold on Niko. I mean, this is the first time I have been in the water since that day. I am not sure exactly what turns me, or what turned me. Give me some time here," said Kris confidently.

Niko snorted again and surveyed the river, quiet and calm. Kris let himself sink to the bottom. He held his breath till his survival instincts pushed him upwards, and he popped back up. Kris paddled awkwardly as Niko watched him. His famous *'give me a break'* look invading his face.

"Kris, seriously. This is ridiculous. Let's just go home, change, and go to school," urged Niko.

"Niko there has to be a trick to this. There has to be something I am missing," said Kris, almost more to himself than to his cousin.

Niko appeared fed up. He swam in Kris's direction. He looped one strong arm under his cousins. He started to pull him back to the shoreline. Out of annoyance and protest, Kris tried to move away. It was not easy. He placed his free arm on Niko's shoulder to try and back him off. Suddenly Niko froze, appearing electrified. Within seconds Niko was staring straight ahead, entranced. He was so engrossed he stopped treading water, although his arm was still hooked under his cousins. Suddenly they both began to sink.

Kris kept his grip on Niko, fully believing that now he would need to save him. Both boys began to sink rapidly. Niko was still in a dazed state. Kris began to panic as Niko let out air bubbles from his nose. Kris did not take a deep breath before they sunk. He feared how long he would be able to stay under.

Kris struggled to free his arm from Niko. He was flailing and kicking as Niko stayed still. Niko was strong. In his frozen condition he locked Kris in place. Kris tried to shake him a bit to wake him up, but nothing took effect. Now that Kris had failed to transform in his two prior attempts, he was growing scared as well.

Kris stared at Niko. He could not hold his breath any longer. He let out an underwater scream, in one last attempt to pull Niko to consciousness. After the muffled sound left him, he gulped a huge mouthful of swampy water. Kris felt himself convulse. He sucked in another mouthful, and then another. He worried that this was the end.

After the last gulp of water, Kris felt it. That familiar pain at his neck. He ran his free hand over his gills as his vision grew sharper. Suddenly he felt super human strength. He freed himself from Niko's hold. He looked at Niko, who was now starting to convulse.

Kris immediately pushed Niko to the surface. When Kris placed his head above water he felt like he needed to hold his breath. It happened. Niko was treading water, staring at the top of Kris's head. Niko did not try to pull at him this time. Niko started to speak.

"Kris, I don't know how you did it. When you touched me, you showed me what happened to you. You showed me the cave, the frogs. I saw it," said Niko in amazement.

Kris came up to the surface quickly and pointed his fingers at his own neck. He showed Niko the gills. Niko just stared. His mouth hung wide open. Kris's flesh was separated smoothly on either side of his neck. The skin flapped rhythmically as he literally gasped, and then submerged again.

"I can see it. This is still crazy, but I can see it!" said Niko.

Kris had no clue how to turn himself back, nor how to communicate in words to Niko. Then he had an idea. He swam to the rocky offshoot and pointed at it. He gestured for Niko to sit.

Niko scrambled on to the rock. Kris touched Niko's hand. Suddenly Niko could fully see Kris underwater, strong and skilled. Kris was breathing freely through his gills. He stared at Niko from under the water. Then Kris started speaking under the surface. Niko could hear him on land because their hands were touching.

"Niko, this is it. Somehow when we sank, it happened. You have to trust me now. I need to get to the cave," Kris explained.

"Cousin, I have an idea," said Niko as their hands were clasped. "What if I get a raft and shadow you? Maybe I can help or something," suggested Niko.

"I do not have much time. Plus, I still need to figure out how to turn back. I promised Blue I would be there today," continued Kris.

Niko's protective instincts kicked in. "I do not want to leave you Kris. I mean… this seems dangerous to me."

"I understand. It's all new for me. Just know that I will be back. I know I will. I swear that I will tell you everything," said Kris in a promising tone.

"OK. I will hang around the river. Maybe that's the best thing to do. I do not know what else to do. This is so cool!" exclaimed Niko.

"OK. Thanks Niko," said Kris as he suddenly let go and did an underwater backflip with the ease of a seal.

CHAPTER TEN

KRIS GLIDED SMOOTHLY through the river. He noticed the intricacy of fallen branches, and the magical patterns of silvery fish. The sun shone brightly through the water. It lit all the shades of green underneath, illuminating the plant life at the base of the river. The bottom of the river was beautiful and relaxing. The landscape reminded him of a dream he once had when he was five years old. In that dream he was able to swim like a fish. Kris forgot about that dream. Then Kris recalled a giant tank of silvery minnows his mom gave him when he was only three years old. He would watch the silvery fish dart around balls of green moss, and swim in and out of small structures he placed inside the aquarium.

Although Kris had only been to the cave once, he remembered exactly where to go. He easily spied the rocky underwater entrance. He swam inside in search of Blue.

As he moved deeper into the structure, he saw Blue sitting on a jagged piece of rock. Blue was waiting in silence for the meeting.

Kris smiled as he looked at Blue. "I am here now Blue," he started.

"Yes human," said Blue with a look of peace. "Now that you have joined the fight, we must hold an initiation."

"Huh?" said Kris, taken aback by the start of their conversation.

"Warriors must be recognized, ritualized, and transformed into an amphibian skin. You have talents far beyond your knowledge. Now we will bestow our armor on you human," said Blue.

Suddenly Blue let out a mighty croak. In an instant an army of frogs waded forth, flanking him on both sides. Kris noticed the distinctive Green frogs first. They let out short, explosive, banjo-pluck calls which they linked together like a series of echoes.

Then Kris saw the Pickerel frogs. They let out snoring, belly-growl calls as they approached. Kris was surprised to see Leopard frogs in the mix. The Leopard frog's staccato version of the Pickerel frog growl, mixed with chuckling grunts, filled his ears.

Blue signaled to the Green frogs first. A serious looking Green frog swam face to face with Kris as Blue spoke. "Green frogs have a fascinating weapon. They are able to lower the dominant frequency of their calls. This makes the enemy believe they are larger than their actual size."

Kris stared at the frogs. He remained motionless, not sure what Blue would say or do next. Suddenly Kris was surrounded by a mass of Green frogs that seemed to appear from nowhere. In unison they let out a deafening croak that echoed in Kris's ears mercilessly. Kris motioned to cover his ears. He did not notice the proximity of the smallest Green frog to his head. As he moved his hands to block his ears, he shoved the tiny frog into his ear.

Suddenly Kris began to writhe. He was pained by the intruder, and frantic to get him out of his ear. Blue and the others stared on, knowing this was part of the ritual. Kris twisted from side to side, clearly experiencing unimaginable discomfort. Suddenly Kris let out a croak identical to that of the Green frog. A croak of aggression and defense. Once this happened the little Green frog popped free from his ear.

Kris, still in pain, let out another defensive croak. This time the sound was strong enough to blow the Green frogs backwards in the water. Blue smiled at the power the boy displayed. He could now mimic a type of frog, fool an enemy, and project a larger stature.

Kris looked around to see the frogs watching him. Blue continued "Pickerel frogs are particularly difficult to catch and hold on to. This is due to their slippery, toxic skin secretions. They also have impressive leaping ability."

Kris looked on as a threatening group of Pickerel frogs approached him skillfully. All at once they seemed to leap through the water. They made their way under Kris's shirt. The skins of the frogs felt like tiny needles, piercing through Kris's skin and stinging his flesh.

Kris winced, convulsed, and grabbed forcefully at his shirt. His gesture was futile. He could not free the Pickerel frogs from his skin. They seemed glued to him. As Kris endured the pain, his movements in the water seemed to grow sharper and quicker. Suddenly he bent his legs and produced a mighty leap. He rocketed forward into a small group of fish. His hand brushed one of the fishes as he moved, leaving a mark of injury on the unlucky passerby.

His eyes opened in amazement. He now understood why the frogs needed to see him, and what they were doing. In the most magical way, they were passing their powers to him. Kris leapt through the water again, more controlled this time. He floated in front of Blue, looking as graceful as the frogs.

Suddenly the group of Pickerel frogs let out a loud croaking cheer. They leapt, did somersaults, and paddled with joy. Blue also released a joyous croak.

"Fellow amphibians, we are off to a good start," said Blue. "Leopard frogs use crypsis. They are some of the most powerful when it comes to camouflage. They avoid detection from their enemies this way."

As Blue spoke, a group of Leopard frogs approached Kris. Before Kris knew it, they surrounded him on all sides. With their bodies, they formed a cone-like shape around him. Then they began to swim remarkably fast all in one direction, creating a miniature tornado effect. Kris felt himself spin around inside the cone of frogs. He noticed flashes of color within the swirling water. Just as he was beginning to feel dizzy, the movement stopped and the frogs dispersed. Kris looked at his bare arms and hands. He saw they were dappled with the colors of the underwater branches, green plants, and even gray rock.

Kris smiled. He felt as joyous as the frogs. Blue continued "human, these powers are just small gifts. Offerings to bring you luck in the battle. You must know that the gifts we have provided you today do not compare to those already sealed in your bones … those that have come from a more powerful place. You have already discovered that you are a water and land breather. Your awareness of this came through struggle. Let us hope that the discovery of your full powers comes through calmer channels."

The frogs cheered again. Beautiful pitched croaks filled the water as Blue waited in silence.

"Blue, tell me about the battle. I still do not understand it," said Kris.

Blue nodded as the frogs grew silent. Their wide eyes stared at Kris. They now seemed to hang in the water motionless, as if they were suspended in time.

"Human, billions of years ago the fight for planet earth began. The earliest inhabitants were mighty reptiles. They died in a terrible battle," began Blue.

"You are speaking of dinosaurs, right?" asked Kris.

Blue nodded in agreement, and continued "the alien force gained footing during that time. Our kind went into hiding, but survived. The earth suffered damage from the fighting. The meteor attacks made the planet less appealing. The aliens knew only long periods of time could recover it. The alien forces spread across the galaxy. They perfected distant moons, preparing for the time when they would return to earth in full force. They also stationed some troops on earth. Clever, invisible, and masters of deceit … they found a way to penetrate this planet and observe. All the while entirely unknown."

Kris was taken aback, unsure of how this could be. "Blue, I bet that if the aliens were living among people now, someone would spot them. I mean, they must be different from humans. You just need to look," said Kris assuredly.

"Human, are you saying that all humans are alike?" said Blue.

"Well, yeah. I mean, of course we have different skin color, hair color, nationalities. You know, all those things," said Kris.

"You speak of human outer skins. We frog have them as well, with brilliant variation. But consider this, would not human skin be the perfect disguise then?" asked Blue.

Kris was speechless as he stared at Blue, entirely stunned by the notion that aliens could disguise themselves so ingeniously. "But Blue, to have human skin, they would need to murder humans!" Kris said.

"No, not at all. These aliens are clever, deceitful creatures. They save pain for war, which makes them all the more powerful," said Blue.

"But there is not a skin store they can go to. I don't understand how they can wear skin and disguise themselves," Kris said.

"They invade," replied Blue, a solemn look on his small frog face.

Kris stared in disbelief, still confused by how any of this could be possible.

"They pick the smallest of victims. Those whose minds have not formed adult thoughts. Those who do not have the power of speech."

Blue swam up close to Kris and said "put your hand on my head."

Kris robotically placed his hand on top of Blue's head. He saw a flash of light, then a playground. He saw a small child playing alone, lining up sticks and rocks. Suddenly he saw another child on a swing, solitary and staring towards the trees. Then he saw a bright classroom with a teacher sitting across from a speechless child. The teacher was holding up objects and saying "point to…"

Kris removed his hand rapidly. He faced Blue and said "this is crazy."

Blue stared at Kris, entirely calm. "You see human, the alien has been indistinguishable, hasn't he? There are truly children who cannot speak. Children who have real challenges and carry genes for autism, mutism, and other things that stop them from producing sounds. And then there are some children who have none of those authentic issues. These children were simply picked randomly to serve as conduits."

"This is horrible Blue. This cannot be true!" Kris said in a frightened tone.

"Clever, masterful. The alien chose to blend among a sub-group of children. You see, once invaded the alien simply puts a human's mind on hold. This allows the alien to walk among the earth and observe the best battlegrounds. Children spend time in zoos, at lakes, beaches, and playing outdoors. They do not have to work. They get their nutrition from an adult source. They need not worry about shelter. The aliens can roam battlegrounds, gain information, and plan their attack. Of course, they must contend with school. That's the easy part. Since they cannot speak English easily, they simply do not speak. They are often mistaken for special children because of that," explained Blue.

Kris felt a sadness growing inside him. He looked at the frogs around him. They had worried expressions on their faces. Kris looked back to Blue.

"So human, this is how they hide. They are coming to the earth in greater numbers, disguised as children," Blue said.

"How do we stop this?" asked Kris.

"Through cleverness, creativity, and the most powerful mind," said Blue. "The mind of a child."

Suddenly Kris felt a strange prickling in his neck. He immediately processed his survival instinct. He held his breath. He rocketed to the surface of the water in what felt like two seconds, thanks to his frog abilities.

Kris popped to the surface. He opened his mouth wide, and let the sweet air in. He looked to the left, then to the right, for the translator. He noticed nothing but Niko fifteen feet away on a canoe.

"Kris," Niko yelled, overjoyed to see him as he paddled himself over. "I went to the house and lugged this old thing here. I have been paddling all over this river for hours and hours. It's six o'clock."

"Niko, did you notice anything strange right before I came up?" said Kris eagerly.

Niko cocked his head and replied "Ah…. Kris, this whole thing is strange!"

"I mean, did you see something. Someone out of the ordinary near the water?"

Niko closed his eyes. "Well the sky seemed a little brighter. I almost put my sunglasses back on to stop the glare, but then I guess a cloud came."

Kris looked to the sky to see no clouds in sight. "Thanks Niko, that's helpful," he said.

"Well, what the heck happened down there?" asked Niko.

"Niko, I saw that frog again. He explained why the frogs are so scared. There is a battle coming. Between some kind of alien and earth."

Niko shook his head, as if clearing it. "Kris, you are now saying that there are aliens from outer space coming?"

"Niko, they are actually here. Right here among us. They are just waiting to attack," explained Kris.

"That sounds really crazy cousin. Maybe you got it wrong," said Niko.

"Niko, they disguise themselves as kids," said Kris seriously.

A look of panic invaded Niko's face. "We need to tell the police. We need to tell someone," Niko exclaimed.

"It would not help Niko. Blue said the only one to fight this battle is a person with a child's mind. There is something critical about the warrior being a kid," said Kris.

Niko stared in amazement. He was trying to process everything Kris had to say. He watched Kris hop into the canoe with one swift leap. He had never seen his cousin move so powerfully before.

"Besides, no one would believe us. We would wind up in a special school on a truckload of medications if we tried to convince any adult of this. People would think we were crazy. But you know this is real Niko. We both know it is real," said Kris seriously.

Kris and Niko sat in the canoe silently as they thought about the strange situation they were now in. The sun was setting in the sky.

"My mom, does she have a clue Niko?" asked Kris.

"Nope. I phoned your house and told her that we were signing up for an after-school homework club. It gets out around now. We are in the clear," said Niko proudly.

"Thanks Niko. Thanks for helping me," said Kris.

"So, what are we going to do?" said Niko, his voice desperate.

"Let's make a plan after supper. We need to get back to one of the houses fast. We need to make sure no one suspects anything."

CHAPTER ELEVEN

K RIS AND NIKO went to their respective houses. Both kids dodged as many questions as they could about the 'homework club' Niko claimed they joined. After Kris ate dinner, he asked "so since my homework is done, can I go to Niko's?"

His mother looked quizzical for a moment. She decided that a visit would be fine. Her only request was that Kris tidy up his room first. Kris knew better than to protest over such a minor point as picking up his room, when the goal was to just get to Niko. The boys lived close. Getting to Niko's would take under fifteen minutes. Kris would be there in no time.

Kris called Niko on the phone to confirm the gathering. Niko's mom was militant. Once Niko finished talking his aunt took the phone over. She demanded to speak to Kris.

"So … what homework did you guys finish?" she asked Kris in a doubting tone.

"Auntie, we did our math and science. Pages 42-58 in math. We wrote a lab on observing leaves, and the color changes they undergo," said Kris.

Kris's aunt was silenced. Kris was the kind of kid that knew assignments in advance. It was easy for him to rattle off what needed to be attended to, even two weeks in advance. Kris could only hope that Niko did not contradict the story he was currently telling his aunt.

"Well, you boys can hang out for just a little while," his aunt started, "and I want you both to practice your cursive writing before you leave."

"OK auntie. I will bring extra lined paper in case you guys don't have enough," Kris added for good measure.

Kris's mother tried not to laugh as she heard her son negotiate with his over-strict aunt. Although Kris was talking to her sister, they had markedly different views on school, child development, and what childhood should be. Kris frowned as he hung up the phone.

"All set sweetheart?" Kris's mother said as she watched him hang up the phone.

"Yeah, Auntie Lisa is making us do cursive. I already know cursive mom," Kris said.

"I know honey. You will end up using it at a minimum as an adult. Probably just to sign a check, like most people – including your aunt!" added his mother.

"I know mom. It's too much. Poor Niko," said Kris. The two then stood up and gathered their jackets. Kris's mom hugged him as they turned to walk out the door.

CHAPTER TWELVE

IKO'S HOUSE WAS very large and always very clean. His mother was a full time housewife. Kris's mother worked more hours than any mother should have to. She was his sole parent. Niko had two teenage sisters. The girls were usually consumed with their social network, academic endeavors, and gossip of the day. Based on this, the girls typically were out of sight. Niko also had two little dogs who loved to bark at strangers and family members with equal zeal.

Kris and his mom entered Aunt Lisa's kitchen. Kris waved his lined paper and two pencils in the air upon seeing his aunt, to show her that he was serious about the handwriting work-out. On cue, the two dogs started barking right away. It was as if there was a major break in, and the very lives of the family were being threatened.

Unphased by all the noise, Niko was sitting at the kitchen table. He was asking his mother for brownies.

"Come on mom. I ate all my chicken and I am still hungry," he whined.

"Why not try a fruit pop, an apple, or some soy nuts?" she countered. She was trying to steer him from the brownie and into a fat free nutrition lane.

Kris walked over to Niko and discreetly pointed to his backpack. His aunt was too busy scanning the fridge for another nutritious proposal to notice Kris's gesture.

"Ah forget it mom," Niko said quickly as he scurried off with Kris. The boys left the two mothers in the kitchen alone.

"All they want to eat is junk. Its nutrition or nothing in this house," exclaimed Niko's mom with a nod towards her sister. "Tonight at least he saw the light and gave up before badgering me into a coma. I should make a sign that reads *nutrition or nothing*. I like the sound of that."

Kris's mom laughed. Her sister would likely make that sign. "Yeah. Well, when it matters to the boys they will be as body conscious as the girls. Wait and see," said Kris's mom pensively. "Time is flying, you know. It seems like yesterday that they were only five and trying that soccer class," she added.

"It seems like yesterday they were only two," Lisa countered. Then she realized the statement she just made. A look of regret filled her eyes. "I am sorry. That slipped out. None of us will ever forget that time in your lives. I was just throwing out a quick number to add to what you were saying. I am a moron."

Kris's mom sat quietly. A memory of Kris at age two surfaced in her mind. Lisa was not a malicious person. She would never try to conjure that time period on purpose. Kris's mother pushed the memory of the pool out of her mind. That terrible memory that all the adults worked so hard to forget.

"It's behind us," said Lisa. Then she quickly added "want some tea?" as she rapidly took out cups. Kris's mother smiled. She was going to drink the tea even if she wasn't in the mood. The sisters continued to talk about better subjects. The sound of their voices faded out as Kris and Niko went to the basement to see if they could claim unoccupied territory. They were delighted to see that the girls had abandoned their Wii work-outs.

Kris took out some homemade brownies and the paper. Kris could multitask easily. He started the writing for good measure. Niko started as well. He knew that once his aunt left, his mom would make a round or two.

"Thanks for the snacks man," said Niko.

"We are growing boys," said Kris as he looked over his shoulder. He wanted to make sure they were really alone.

"Let's get down to business," said Niko as he scooted closer to Kris. "Have you thought more about the aliens?"

"I have not stopped thinking about them. From what I learned, Blue said that the aliens disguise themselves as kids. The important part is that they never speak," explained Kris.

"Kind of like the kids in room 24?" said Niko.

"Maybe. Hard to tell. I mean, there are kids that really have problems speaking, and then there are the aliens. Blue did say that they need to invade a young mind. So … I do not think that the kids our age in room 24 really sound right. Maybe they are too old," said Kris.

"I get it. So, it's really little kids. Like the ones in kindergarten or something," surmised Niko.

"I guess. I mean, they are young and all," said Kris.

"Kris, even if we locate an alien … what exactly are we supposed to do about it?" inquired Niko.

"I have no clue. I really am stuck. I mean, the little kids are sort of possessed. It's not like they, the actual kid, is the problem here," said Kris.

"I know. It's not their fault. They maybe do not even know," added Niko.

"So maybe it's just knowing how to tell the difference. Or maybe getting a count. To plan a defense for what could come. Maybe we could follow an alien to see what it's doing. Does that make sense?" asked Kris.

"Yeah. It's like spying. Seeing what they are planning. But how are we supposed to hang out with these little kids?" wondered Niko.

"There must be a way to do this. You know how sometimes the girls go read books to younger classes?" Kris said.

"Yeah, the girls get to the little kids all the time that way. What a great idea!" said Niko emphatically.

"Maybe that's the ticket in," said Kris with a smile.

Niko looked excited as he whispered "you are so smart, good one Kris."

"So tomorrow, let's see what we can do about volunteering to read. Maybe we can do something else as well," Kris whispered back.

"OK Kris," said Niko. A smile of excitement lit his face.

Suddenly the boys heard footsteps on the stairs. Niko impulsively shoved the remaining brownies in his mouth. He picked up his pencil as his mom rounded the corner.

"Good job boys. You got to practice. Homework is good. It will make you smarter," Lisa said as she rounded the corner.

Niko was chewing on the brownie, trying not to laugh. His mother moved out as quickly as she moved in, satisfied that progress was being made.

CHAPTER THIRTEEN

THE NEXT DAY Kris woke early. He was eager to get to school in order to *really* make-up for his missed work. Kris was an early bird like his mom. He felt most productive when he woke up with the sun.

His mother, on the other hand, woke up late. She had a scary dream. It was triggered by the conversation she had with her sister the night before. She dreamt of screaming Kris's name, then finding his little body at the bottom of the big pool. She dove in head first at the speed of light to rescue him. In the dream, she was trying to grab her son, but he kept slipping through her hands.

In reality, Kris did not slip through his mother's hands. By the power of a miracle, Kris was OK. He went on with no memory of what really happened that day. Kris was saved. He had no memories of the coma, or of what he used to say immediately following his awakening. He only knew that his mom was always smiling at him when he was a toddler. She was always telling him to wish on the brightest stars, because wishes come true.

Kris's mom was quickly packing his snack and multi-tasking to make up for the late start. Before they both knew it, Kris was on his way to school and his mom was on her way to work. The morning seemed to fly by.

Kris started his day with the usual. Journal work, math, literacy block, recess, lunch, social studies, and then free block. Free block was a time when kids went to instrument lessons, stayed in to work, or some of the girls went to read. Normally Kris stayed in to work. He loved soaking in the time, but today he approached Ms. Christine instead.

"Ms. Christine, I was wondering if I could volunteer to read to the little kids in kindergarten?"

Ms. Christine looked thrilled, probably because someone other than a girl finally asked for this responsibility.

"Why Kris, what a great idea. You would make a terrific role model for the boys. And you are an excellent reader. Why don't you run along with Reta and Linda?"

"Thanks Ms. Christine," Kris said with a smile. He quickly turned to head to the kindergarten wing. He could only hope Niko was as successful. He did not see Niko in the hall that led to the kindergarten wing. He knew this was a bad sign.

Kris picked up his pace. He hoped Niko was already in the kindergarten class. As he entered the room he saw Reta and Linda. They were browsing the bookshelf. No signs of Niko.

The cheery kindergarten teacher, Mr. John, approached Kris with his hand positioned for a high five.

"Ms. Christine just called and told me the good news. Great to have you here buddy," he said as he slapped his open palm to Kris's.

"It's good to be here. I am not sure what to do. Just let me know and I will jump in," said Kris.

"Right now, we are just cleaning up. We are getting ready for story time. You can help by helping the kids put back the toys. You might notice that some of the kids need some extra help. You can show them how it's done, and they just might copy you."

"Thanks for explaining it to me," said Kris as his eyes wandered around the room. It was hard to tell which kids were not talking, or which kids to try and observe. Kris made his way to the block area. He figured he would try small talk as a method to narrow down possible aliens.

Kris noticed a small boy with light brown hair and blue eyes. The boy was not cleaning up. Instead he was lining up blocks in a pattern. "Hi, I'm Kris," he said as he sat beside the boy. The boy did not look up or answer. The child kept on playing. "We need to clean up now. I can help you." Kris motioned to pick up a block. The boy, quick as lightning, stretched out his hand and halted Kris. For a moment Kris was stunned. How could he move that fast? What was so important about the block pattern?

"Are you making a building?" asked Kris in a cheerful tone.

"Space station," the boy said without looking up.

Suddenly Mr. John appeared and said "James, it's time to put the blocks away. Will you put away five or ten blocks?"

James responded by quietly saying "five blocks."

"Kris will get the rest. Count five, and then go to the rug," added Mr. John.

James robotically counted five. He carefully placed the blocks on the small shelf as a perfect stack, then went to the rug. He never glanced at Kris. The whole interaction was trickier than Kris expected. This kid could speak, but he moved so fast and said "space station."

Kris felt confused. He whispered *focus* to himself as he went to the circle to hear Linda read to the class.

Reta was sitting beside a dark haired, plump girl. The girl held a little squishy ball in her hand. She rocked back and forth. As Linda read, the girl smiled intensely. She also made unintelligible noises, and fidgeted. Kris noticed that from time to time Reta held up a small card. The card showed a mouth with a circle around it. There was a big red line across the circle. When Reta showed the girl the card she stopped fidgeting. The girl also grew quieter.

Linda finished the story and started asking some easy questions. She asked the class "what kind of animal was in the book?"

Kris noticed that the girl beside Reta did not try to answer, or raise a hand. Reta was using picture cards of animals. She was asking her to point to the correct animal to answer the question. Kris thought maybe he found a no talker. He watched intently.

Mr. John made his way to the center of the rug. He asked the class to thank Linda for the story. The time seemed to go by quickly. Kris had forgotten that Niko was not even there. Mr. John then personally thanked Linda, Reta, and Kris. "See you next week," he exclaimed as he waved a cheerful goodbye.

Kris exited the room behind the girls. They seemed glued together as they scurried off to the bathroom. He walked about five feet behind them. Kris felt hopeful but worried. How could he let another week pass? There had to be a way to connect with more little kids, but how?

Suddenly Kris saw Niko exit the bathroom. "Hey, what happened?" said Kris as he saw Niko.

"Had to stay in for our free block. I am way behind from yesterday," said Niko in an exasperated tone.

"Oh darn. I forgot about you making up school work. Niko, sorry about that," said Kris.

"Well … spill it bro," said Niko eagerly.

"OK, it was fast. I only noticed one person that did not talk. It was a girl, which is weird because I thought non-talkers would be boys for some reason."

"Do you think the girl lost her voice to aliens?" Niko whispered.

"I have no idea. No idea at all. But there must be a way to tell. I think that I need to spend a lot of time with these little kids," said Kris.

"When I asked my teacher if I could do kindergarten volunteers … she gave me a big, fat 'no, do your make-up work'. Then she mentioned something else Kris," said Niko.

"Yeah. Go on," prodded Kris.

"She said that if I wanted to help so badly, I should volunteer for an extended daytime position. They need good role models to help the huge amount of kids," said Niko.

"Obviously she does not know you so well," said Kris with a smile. "But seriously Niko, that's perfect … way better than story time. Longer for sure."

"OK, looks like we have a plan," Niko said excitedly.

"Yes. Let's get ourselves signed up for volunteering after school, and let's get to the bottom of things," said Kris with a gleam in his eye.

CHAPTER FOURTEEN

IMMEDIATELY AFTER SCHOOL Kris and Niko went to the Extended Day room. They asked if they could use some volunteers. Extended day was split into two levels. One level was kids from kindergarten to grade two. The other level had kids from grade three to grade five. Anyone could go. Kids from all types of different classes and programs attended.

The little kids' class was staffed with a group of young teachers who looked more like camp counselors. The head teacher seemed a little older than the rest of the staff. Her name was Ms. Lori. The boys approached her.

"Um, hi. Me and my cousin are looking to volunteer with little kids. Do you have any kindergartners in after school?" Kris asked Ms. Lori.

Ms. Lori beamed, clearly glad to have volunteers. "Well, this is terrific guys. We do not see that many boys ... I mean kids … your age volunteering after school. And we do have some little kids here. I bet they would love to play with you."

Niko looked at Kris out of the corner of his eye. He gave Kris a nod. Kris winked back.

"Boys, do your parents know you are here helping us out?" asked Ms. Lori.

"Uh, yeah. My mom works so she is not home after school. She will be glad that I have something other than T.V. to do," said Kris quickly.

"Same here," Niko lied.

"OK, then it looks like we are all set here. Have fun!" said Ms. Lori. She turned quickly. Her bouncy chestnut hair fell over her left shoulder as she swung her head back in the direction of the counselors. Kris waited a moment to see if she would acknowledge he and Niko again, or give them instructions. After a few minutes it was clear they would be on their own.

"OK, here we go," whispered Kris. "Look for little kids that do not talk."

"Roger that," said Niko. They spread out, making their way through a large room crowded with children from younger grades.

Kris felt badly that so many kids had to be in after school. Kris always loved the comfort of going home. He loved relaxing on his comfortable couch. He loved his homemade snacks from his mom, which were always waiting for him upon arrival. He also loved the freedom to watch T.V., or read a fun book. These kids had to play with only the toys in the room. They could not curl up on a couch with a blanket and hot chocolate after school.

Kris noticed that the girl with the picture cards was sitting quietly in a corner looking at a book. There was a teacher with her. The teacher was a young woman that Kris had seen in the halls before. The young woman occasionally covered a teacher's absence. She also randomly covered recess duty. This young teacher was staring out the window, lazily flipping a key ring of picture cards in her hands. She seemed to be spaced out.

"Uh, hello," Kris said to the young teacher and little girl. "I'm Kris, a new volunteer."

The young teacher looked at Kris as if she did not want to be bothered by noise. A long silence followed his introduction, which Kris decided to fill.

"What book are you reading?" he asked the girl.

The teacher seemed to spring to life at the question. "Daria does not speak, so she cannot answer you. She needs to communicate through pictures and things like that," said the teacher flatly.

Daria seemed to be listening. She glanced at Kris. Then she tilted her book towards him. This act seemed to surprise the teacher. "You can read to her, she likes that," added the teacher quickly, her face turning a shade of red.

As Kris motioned to touch the book he said "Daria, I would like to read to you." Daria glanced at him again and shifted the book closer to Kris. The teacher looked even more surprised.

"My name is Ione," said the teacher, "you can *only* call me that here in the after school program. If you see me in a classroom, or even in the halls during the day, you must call me Ms. Pimple," she said with a tone of absolute seriousness.

Kris was biting his tongue trying not to laugh. How in the world does anyone get the last name Pimple? She said it so seriously too. He felt like he was being pranked. As he looked at her he thought that any minute she would say she was only kidding. After a few obvious seconds that this was not a joke, he pushed his urge to laugh out of his mind. He turned his attention back to Daria.

Kris gently placed Daria's book on his lap. He sat next to the quiet girl. She looked so sweet and trusting. Kris started to read a story about a little mouse going on a big adventure. Daria stared at the pictures as Kris read the story.

In the meantime, Niko zeroed in on a little boy playing with puzzles. This little boy also had a teacher with him. Niko knew the teacher from the times she would bring the boy around school to help do 'teacher jobs.' He did things like deliver attendance, or the lunch count. Suddenly a loud shriek came from the direction of Niko and the boy.

"I … I am sorry. I was just trying to show Max where to place that puzzle piece," Niko stammered.

"Max has his own system. It's hard for him to share his puzzle. He is OK. He does not say many words. Sometimes when he is frustrated he yells," said Ms. Stephanie.

"I really am sorry. Max, I really am," said Niko, clearly shaken by the fact that Max was so upset with him.

"Niko, it's OK. Max just has a different way of communicating, that's all," continued Ms. Stephanie.

"OK, I am going to check on my cousin. Thanks for explaining," said Niko as he backed away from Max, who had an angry look on his face.

Niko came over to Kris and Daria and sat down. Ione seemed to not notice him. Instead she resumed her spaced out window look. Kris finished the book and smiled at Daria, who sat very quietly.

"Bye Daria, it was fun reading to you," Kris said as he stood up and motioned for Niko to walk with him.

When Kris and Niko were in an uncrowded area, Kris whispered "what did you do to that kid?"

"Nothing. I just picked up a puzzle piece and he got mad at me," said Niko defensively.

Kris closed his eyes to concentrate. "Did you notice anything about that kid? Anything strange?"

"Apart from the fact that he would not let me touch the puzzle?" said Niko.

"Yeah. You know, something that might lead us to think he was one of the people the aliens took over?" said Kris.

"Not really. Kris, here's the thing … we do not have a clue about how to identify which non-talking kids are possessed by aliens."

"Niko, something must make them identifiable. Something has to be different," said Kris in a frustrated tone.

"Uh, Kris, couldn't your frog friend have given you more specifics?" asked Niko.

"I ran out of time underwater. I mean …. maybe he could have," said Kris.

As Kris and Niko spoke, they saw a boy being escorted into the room. The teacher was right by his side. Both Kris and Niko recognized this kid. His name was Albie. Sometimes Albie would come to music class with a teacher. Albie often got angry about something. He was known to throw things. Albie liked to play alone on the playground. Sometimes he tried to scale the fence. Albie seemed big and strong. He was not anyone to mess with.

"What about Albie?" asked Niko.

"I never have seen him long enough to know if he talks. He always seems to get mad at something and leaves class early," said Kris.

"I once saw Albie reading a note from a teacher. He must read," added Niko.

Albie's teacher, Ms. Dora, was bright and cheerful. She was one of the friendlier adults at the school. She immediately recognized the boys. After she got Albie seated and working with some Legos, she came over to Kris and Niko.

"Hey boys, good to see you here!" she announced.

"Thanks Ms. Dora. We are volunteers," said Niko.

"Cool, so is Albie. He really likes little kids," Ms. Dora beamed.

Kris and Niko looked at each other, then at Ms. Dora, with complete surprise. They only knew Albie through his reputation for throwing, and subsequent removal from class.

"Ms. Dora, how does Albie volunteer here?" asked Niko.

"Well, lots of people do not know it but Albie is a pro builder. He also makes beautiful pictures. He is able to model how to do certain things. The little kids can learn how to make things by watching him demonstrate," she said proudly.

"Oh, we do not know Albie that well. He keeps to himself a lot on the playground. We never see him at lunch," added Kris.

"Well, he could stand some new friends," said Ms. Dora hopefully. "Would you like to say hello to him?"

Kris knew that Ms. Dora was pressing some type of introduction. Albie really intimidated Kris. He felt nervous. Kris froze into place and waited for Niko to respond. Niko stared at his shoes waiting for Kris to say something.

"Come on guys. Albie is really a cool kid," she added.

"OK," Niko finally said.

"Right this way," Ms. Dora said as she led the way to the Lego area where Albie was bent over.

"Albie, this is Kris and Niko," said Ms. Dora to Albie's bent head. Albie was busy quickly clicking Lego's together. He did not look up.

"Albie, time to look at Kris and Niko and wave hello," said Ms. Dora.

Kris and Niko were surprised to see Albie look up and wave. His steel gray eyes shot through them momentarily. Within seconds he resumed his Lego work.

Ms. Dora looked at the boys, who were still surprised Albie even looked at them. "Now is a good time to say hello boys," Ms. Dora suggested in an urgent whisper.

"Oh right," said Kris.

"Hello," both boys said in unison. Albie continued to look downwards. Niko and Kris fought the urge to say 'jinx'.

"He hears you," said Ms. Dora, "even though it's hard for him to look and hear you at the same time. Albie is a very smart guy. He is working on ways to show people, right Albie?" she said to the bent head.

"Ms. Dora, does Albie talk?" Niko whispered.

"Not really. He understands us. Talking is hard and he gets frustrated easily," Ms. Dora said quietly.

Suddenly Ms. Dora's voice was loud again "Albie has a great new computer, brand new. It has all sorts of words on it. Albie, let's show the kids what it can do," said Ms. Dora happily. She quickly rummaged through a large blue bag and retrieved a square shaped box.

"Albie has been practicing how to use this computer. It's called a Dynavox. It's really neat. Albie, let's show the kids your favorite page," said Ms. Dora as she handed it to Albie.

Albie stared at the computer as if lost in some kind of thought. "Albie, now it's time to press a joke," said Ms. Dora.

Suddenly Albie's long finger extended and pressed a button. Everyone heard "why did the skeleton go to the doctor's office?"

"Uh, beats me," said Niko.

"I don't know Albie. Maybe to get some medicine?" said Kris.

Albie then pressed another button. "To get a booooster shot," the computer said in a robotic voice.

Niko and Kris laughed, as did Ms. Dora. Albie did not laugh. He was still staring at the talking box.

"This is a way Albie can communicate," said Ms. Dora excitedly.

Suddenly Albie picked up the box and flipped it over. He was pulling at it, as if trying to open it up. "Albie, that was good work. Time for a break," said Ms. Dora.

Albie automatically stopped pulling at the computer. He looked at Ms. Dora with those cold eyes. Ms. Dora pulled out a bullseye caramel candy and handed it to Albie. Albie quickly took off the wrapping and ate it. He then squished together the fingers on both hands and pressed his left and right fingertips together.

"That is sign language for more," said Ms. Dora. She quickly gave Albie another bullseye.

"Thanks for showing us your computer," said Kris to Albie. Ms. Dora quickly taught Kris and Niko sign language for the word 'thank you'. The boys made the gesture to Albie, who looked at them with his steel gray eyes and said nothing.

CHAPTER FIFTEEN

NIKO AND KRIS walked home more puzzled than ever. In between their wonderment, they joked about Ms. Pimple's name. They talked about how they both wanted to yell jinx when they said 'hello' at the same time. They also pondered whether the rules of jinx applied if over an hour had passed and no one called it. After a heated debate on this topic, they turned their attention back to the mission.

"OK. Any of them could be an alien … I think," said Kris.

"But isn't Albie too old?" asked Niko.

"I guess. Unless he's been an alien for a while. Do you think that's possible?" wondered Kris.

"They are all so different," said Niko.

"I know. Daria seems so sweet," said Kris.

"Yeah, plus she's a girl. So how could she be an alien? makes no sense," said Niko, shaking his head.

"Albie is the least friendly, don't you think?" said Kris.

"Well, the way he was staring at us. Like maybe he knew we knew or something?" said Niko.

"Not sure. But that makes sense, Niko."

"Well, you are not the only smart one in the family," said Niko proudly.

"I have another idea," said Kris.

"Oh boy," said Niko.

"Seriously, how can we trail these three?" said Kris.

"What! Are you nuts?" exclaimed Niko.

"No. I mean maybe out of school it's obvious. Maybe one of them is doing strange things," said Kris.

"Well, I guess. I mean an alien should be plotting in some way," said Niko.

"Did you see how Albie tried to open the computer? Maybe he is like E.T. or something. He could be trying to build a phone to talk to the mothership," said Kris.

"Did not think of that. Maybe you are right," Niko said in a serious tone.

"OK. We are going to zero in tomorrow. We are off to a good start though," said Kris as he held up his open palm in front of Niko.

Niko slapped Kris's open palm enthusiastically with his own. Then they each turned in separate directions on the sidewalk, heading home.

CHAPTER SIXTEEN

AS KRIS LAY **in bed he tossed and turned. Finally, he fell into a deep sleep. Kris dreamt that Albie was standing near the edge of a river. He had a wide grin on his face. Suddenly Albie reached into the pocket of his light blue hoodie. He pulled out a small metal ball. He shook it quickly in the air, then tossed it violently into the water. Suddenly the river went up in flames. Albie stood in the fire laughing. Within seconds Albie's human form melted. A skeleton walked away from the fire, still laughing.**

Kris awoke and jumped up in bed. He was sweating, completely disturbed by the dream. Could Albie be at the river right now? Could he be one of the aliens, even though he was older?

As the next few days progressed Kris and Niko continued their volunteer work at the after school program.

They zoned in on Max, Albie, and Daria. They also got more information from their teachers.

They learned that Daria loved to swim. She had a collection of Elmo dolls, and small plastic horses. Max liked to collect sticks. He often would take long nature walks to find sticks to add to his collection. Max's parents took him on many trails. He had been to trails at Walden Pond, and the Charles River. Albie loved the computer. At home one of his favorite pastimes was playing computer games with bright cause and effect actions.

Based on the interests of the kids, Kris and Niko suspected that Albie must be an alien. They reasoned this was possible due to his love of computers. They also felt that Max was suspect because of the long walks. They both doubted Daria could be an alien in disguise. After all, how could girls be aliens anyways?

By Friday Kris and Niko felt like they hit a wall. They were discussing this in the book corner of the after school program, whispering to each other about their mission. Suddenly they noticed a thin blonde woman with strong smelling perfume walk into the room. She wore a gray business suit. Her fingers sparkled with sapphire rings. They were surprised to see the woman approach Albie. With great curiosity they quietly scooted closer to the woman.

"Hi pumpkin. Mommy is so happy to see you having fun," said the woman with a gleaming smile.

Albie looked up and reached out his hand to touch his mothers. Kris and Niko were surprised to see the gesture. Kris smiled at seeing Albie's connection with his mom.

"We have to leave early for your appointment. Are you ready to go?" she asked Albie.

Albie's teacher Ms. Dora piped in "is Albie sick? Because he seems alright. He ate his whole lunch and all his snacks," she said responsibly.

"Oh yes dear. He is not sick. He just has trouble falling asleep at night. Last night he was so awake he left the house. He headed for the direction of the woods. Luckily, we noticed and got to him before he made it too far. I am hoping we can get to the bottom of his sleeplessness."

Kris and Niko stared at each other instantly, a look of enlightenment in their eyes. They watched as Albie's mother took his hand and gathered Albie's belongings. As soon as they left Kris and Niko bolted out of the room and down the hallway.

"Ah ha!" said Kris.

"I knew it," said Niko.

"He must have been heading out to look for information. To plan, to gather materials," said Kris.

"And he can only do it at night so he is not suspicious. So, what are we going to do now, cousin?" asked Niko.

"I think we should trail him," said Kris.

Niko stared in disbelief. "Ah Kris, seriously, you know we can't go out at night. Not even past eight," said Niko.

"Then I will sneak out alone," said Kris resolutely.

"You know my mom. I would be grounded for like, four years or something. We have an alarm in my house. I don't think I can do it," said Niko with a serious tone.

"Then I will do it alone," Kris said calmly.

"When? I mean, come on now!" said Niko, a feeling of panic slipping into his voice.

"Tonight of course. I do not think there is time to waste," said Kris.

The boys were now at the bike rack outside the school. Niko watched Kris lift his bike with one hand so he could better manage the lock. Niko could see Kris was stronger and faster than he had been just a week ago. Kris swiftly unlocked his bike. He started to pedal off, on a mission.

CHAPTER SEVENTEEN

KRIS AND HIS mom had a quiet night. His mother made him a homemade meal. They had breaded chicken cutlets and rice. This was one of Kris's favorite meals. After dinner, Kris and his mom played scrabble. They both had an exceptional vocabulary. Because of this, they loved to create words from the challenge of limited vowels and consonants. As they played they ate popcorn, and had several laughs. As the clock neared nine, Kris's mom yawned a few times.

"Mom, it's alright if you want to go to bed, I can watch a movie or draw," said Kris in a caring tone.

"I am just tired today. Work was long. I guess I did not drink enough coffee," his mother said with a smile as she placed her hand on his shoulder.

Kris instinctively hugged his mom, soaking in her warmth and love. "OK mister, try to remember to turn off the T.V. before you fall asleep," his mom said.

Kris smiled. "I love you mom," he said as she kissed him. "I love you too honey," she replied.

He watched his mom ascend the stairs to her room. Kris then sat on the couch and tried to concentrate on the best way to trail Albie. For starters, he knew Albie lived on Standish Road. He would need to make his way there soon. Kris tried to imagine how he would watch Albie from a distance.

Kris watched the clock. Before he knew it, ten o'clock arrived. He quietly packed a flashlight in his backpack. He also grabbed binoculars, although he was not sure they would work at night. Kris then crept out the door slowly, making sure he had his key.

As he walked down the street he felt the wind sweep up his hair. Feelings of courage flooded through him. He smiled at how brave he was. Albie lived five streets away. Kris knew it would take him roughly twelve minutes to get in the vicinity on foot. As he spied Albie's house he noticed a dim light coming from a top window. He also observed what looked like a bright light and shadows from a T.V. in a downstairs window. Kris figured Albie was upstairs, and that his parents were watching T.V. Kris crouched down behind a mailbox across the street. He figured he would wait there and see what happened.

Within twenty minutes the bottom floor lights went out. The top light stayed on. Kris noticed that another second floor room light went on for roughly four minutes, then it was off. Kris figured this was the parents going to bed. Kris was glowing with his spy skills, and imagined himself working as a CIA agent.

Kris sat for around another forty-five minutes. He fought sleep as he surveyed the house. Suddenly, and with incredible quiet, the front door opened. Albie walked outside. He was wearing his pajamas and slippers. Albie moved quickly in the direction of the woods.

Kris peered around the mailbox. He was amazed that Albie was out of bed and on his own. Steadily he walked a good forty feet behind Albie as they neared the woods. Kris felt a bead of sweat on his neck. He did not think of how strange it would be in the woods this late at night, especially all alone. Kris sped up as Albie neared the edge of the woods. Kris did not know the path Albie was taking, so he did not want to fall too far behind. Luckily, Albie did not notice that Kris was nearing.

Both boys entered the woods. Albie walked without a flashlight to guide him. Kris could hear the branches under Albie's feet. He let the sound of Albie's footsteps guide him. He followed along as quietly as possible. The sound of crickets filled the air.

Kris watched the back of Albie's head in the moonlight. Not once did Albie turn back. Suddenly Kris noticed that Albie made it to the edge of a small body of water. Albie stood silent at the water's edge. He appeared to be looking at the moon.

Kris bent down and watched in fascination, recalling the dream he had about the frogs. Suddenly Kris heard branches snapping somewhere behind him. He felt a sweaty hand over his mouth. Kris kicked backwards and tumbled, fighting to remove the hand. Suddenly he heard "cousin, it's just me, it's Niko."

Kris whipped Niko's hand off his mouth. He spun around to see Niko with his finger to his lips. "How the heck ..." Kris started.

"I couldn't let you have all the fun," Niko said in a frightened whisper. "I have been trailing you since Albie's street. You had no clue!" he said in a superior tone.

"Well, that makes two of us," Kris whispered as he pointed to Albie. Both boys looked at Albie. He was still standing frozen at the water's edge. Albie looked catatonic in the moonlight.

"This is just weird Kris. Maybe he is just sleepwalking. So much for the big doctor appointment after school, huh?" Niko said with a nervous laugh.

Suddenly Kris and Niko heard the sound of fast footsteps falling on the branches, seemingly right behind them. Instinctively both boys dropped and pressed themselves to the forest floor. The sound grew louder. A running foot nearly stepped on Kris's hand. The runner sped towards Albie.

Kris and Niko breathed heavily. They slowly lifted their heads to see what on earth just blew past them. They looked out towards the river, shocked to see Daria standing in the moonlight.

CHAPTER EIGHTEEN

ARIA APPEARED STRONG and steady. She was nothing like the rocking, over-smiley kid in school. She assuredly placed herself in front of Albie and stared into his face. A look of ecstasy could be seen glowing from her eyes in the reflection of the river.

Kris and Niko's mouths hung wide open. They stared straight ahead, completely speechless. Albie let out a moan, which sounded like pain. He suddenly put his hands in the air to shield his face. Daria let out a shrill cry. It was almost birdlike, but clearly unique. She slowly raised her palms towards the sky.

Out of nowhere a swirling gust of wind tore across the river. It whipped the leaves and branches furiously into the air. The air temperature dropped as the eerie howling filled the water's edge. Daria remained in place. She was unshaken by the winds around her. Albie fell to the ground, a muffled cry in his throat.

The temperature continued to plummet. A thin layer of ice stretched across the edge of the river nearest Daria and Albie. Albie remained motionless on the ground. He looked frozen on the now icy leaves and branches. Daria lowered her arms and stared at Albie. She then spoke a dialect unintelligible to Kris and Niko. A series of strange sounds, interspersed with clicks, exploded swiftly from her mouth.

Within seconds a milky green beam of light traced over the water's edge. It made its way towards Albie's motionless body. The beam centered itself directly over Albie.

Something that looked like a lightning bolt shot from the sky. It traveled through the center of the beam, then right into Albie's body. Albie shook a few times on the ground, then slowly sat upright.

Daria continued to make a series of strange sounds. She reached towards Albie and pulled him up. Albie stood in front of Daria. He stared into her face. Suddenly Albie emitted a series of strange sounds too.

Kris and Niko listened to the foreign dialect as they lay still in the leaves. Then Daria abruptly stopped communicating. She took Albie by the hand. In a flash she dived through the thin layer of ice right into the river, taking Albie with her.

Niko instantly grabbed Kris's arm and tugged him up. "We need to get out of here NOW!" he shouted as he pulled Kris away from the river and in the direction of the neighborhood.

Kris did not speak. Instead he ran as fast as his legs could carry him. Neither boy looked back. Even when they hit the pavement both boys kept running. Kris and Niko ran straight to Kris's house. They scrambled into Kris's tree house and fell to the floor, panting. It was a good few minutes before either boy could talk.

"Oh my gosh Niko … they got Albie," said Kris.

"That was horrible. That lightning thing hit him," said Niko as he smashed his hands together to simulate the scene.

"I think it enters people that way. It looks like an act of nature, or something. It disguises itself and all. Then it hits," said Kris.

"Yeah, poor Albie. It looked painful. Maybe he was sleepwalking. Maybe Daria … or whatever she is, planned to attack him," said Niko in a horrified tone.

"That makes sense, Niko. I mean, Albie can hardly speak. He was the perfect victim and now they are using him," said Kris.

"What are we going to do Kris? Do you think they sensed us? Knew we saw them? I can't believe a *girl* is an alien," rambled Niko.

"I think if they knew we were there, they would have attacked us. They were more interested in getting in the water," said Kris as a look of fear spread across his face. "Oh no, Blue!" Kris closed his eyes tight in an effort to communicate with Blue, but nothing happened.

"It will be OK," said Niko as he edged closer to his cousin. "I know it will be alright."

Kris wiped a tear from his face as his mind conjured up an image of the frogs being taken by surprise. "Niko, I need to get in touch with Blue," said Kris, half whispering to himself as his mind raced with thoughts of the river.

"I know, I know," said Niko in a steady voice. "Let's get some sleep and make a plan in the morning, OK?"

"You're right Niko. We need to sleep and then think … think hard about what this all means. How could we have missed Daria?" said Kris as he stared into Niko's eyes.

"It was a great disguise. This alien thing is like an actor or something. She looked so innocent. But now we know that girls can be aliens, what a shocker! Now we know what we are dealing with Kris. It was good that we followed Albie. We are learning," said Niko confidently.

"But learning how to stop it is another thing Niko. I … I cannot imagine how we will fight it," said Kris flatly.

CHAPTER NINETEEN

RIS AND NIKO quietly descended the tree house ladder. They snuck into their beds, undetected. Kris laid in silence. He thought about his world, his mother, and the ignorance he enjoyed not long ago.

As Kris lay in bed he noticed that his skin seemed shiny, smooth, and slightly wet. He examined his fingers. He thought they appeared webbed. Kris felt blood surge through his muscles as he tossed and turned. Finally, he passed out.

Kris had what was probably the strangest dream he ever had. In the dream he was at a pool. It was an unbearably hot day. His skin felt like it was drying out. Kris was with his family. Apparently in this dream he was on *the family vacation* he once took with his aunt and cousins.

In the dream Kris decided to dive into the water. Even though he started out diving in a standard sized hotel pool, he found himself swimming through what seemed to be an underwater city. He could see his house, school, and playground. Then somehow the pool water turned into river water. He was swimming along with fish and turtles. The transition from pool to river was totally natural. Kris felt a sense of calm and peacefulness in the dream. He also experienced a longing to keep exploring the water. As the dream progressed, the wildlife in the water could talk to him. They asked him how he liked it under the surface. Before Kris could answer he found himself in an ambulance. He was speeding towards a hospital. Then Kris woke up. He wondered if any of that was ever real.

Morning seemed to come fast. As Kris emerged from sleep, he was not surprised to hear the sound of Niko's voice downstairs. Niko was talking to his mom. He was putting in his order for breakfast. Kris hurried downstairs to greet him.

"Well, this is a first," said his mom as she flipped a silver dollar pancake on a spatula.

"What time is it mom?" said Kris.

"It's almost 7:30. Don't worry. You are not late at all," his mom replied.

Kris wondered how he could have slept through his alarm. It was set for six. As Kris seated himself his mother placed some pancakes on his plate. She set a bottle of water on the table. "OK boys, I have an early meeting so I will be heading out. Lock up when you go and have a great day," his mom said as she kissed Kris's head and left.

Once the door shut Niko said "I have been up all night thinking about what we should do. I think we should go to after school. We need to see if Albie or Daria appear different."

"Niko, I slept like a rock. Before I went to bed I swear my fingers looked webbed. My skin was almost slimy. I also had a really weird dream about a hotel pool turning into the river. It was that hotel pool we went to when we were kids. From the time we took a family vacation. In the dream I ended up leaving the river in an ambulance," said Kris.

"It's weird you dreamt about that Kris. We were just little kids then. No one ever talks about that vacation except the girls. They always say everyone had a bad time, and we all left early. I don't know if we will ever know why that one trip bombed out," laughed Niko.

"Yeah. It's like something happened and whatever it was is forbidden to speak about. I once asked my mom. She just told me that it was a huge mistake taking that trip. She wouldn't say anything else," said Kris.

The boys felt like they hit a wall with the old vacation conversation. They decided to can the discussion and head to school. When they got to school they noticed some police cars parked out front. Teachers were outside. A van from the local news station was pulling up.

"What the ..." Kris said as they edged in closer. Before they could make their way to the police area, the vice principal approached them. Ms. Sonja was the school's second in command. She was always quick to talk to kids and explain any unusual events.

"Ms. Sonja, what's happening here?" said Niko.

"Boys, one of our students has been reported missing. The police are here to check and see if the student might be in the school somewhere. We are confident that the student is alright. This matter will be settled soon," she said assuredly.

Kris and Niko gave each other a look. Although the vice principal mentioned no names, they already had an idea of who was missing. "Now go on to your class and let the police do their job," she added.

As the boys walked into the school Niko frantically said "it's Albie. He is in that river Kris. We know where he is."

"You are reading my mind Niko. This is getting more serious. Blue was right. We need to think faster, to plan. How about if we meet up at lunch and talk? I can barely think straight right now because everything is happening so fast," said Kris.

"Deal," said Niko as they branched in the hallway.

Kris went to class. He could hardly think about school. His mind kept replaying the events of last night, and the shocking news of the morning. Kris seemed so 'off' that even his teacher asked if he was feeling sick. It was unlike him to be so distant in class. Before he knew it the bell for lunch sounded. He quickly met Niko at their favorite table.

"Kris, how could we have guessed it wrong?" Niko started.

Kris gave him a look of confusion. "What are you talking about Niko?"

"Daria, it's Daria who is missing. Albie is in school. I saw him getting a drink. Daria is the missing kid. Everyone is talking about it. What planet are you on?"

"I have spent the morning thinking. I did not hear anyone talking about it," said Kris earnestly.

"Well now you know," Niko snorted. A look of incredulity on his face. "What are we going to do?"

"We need to get to the river. We need to figure out what's happening," said Kris.

"But Kris you still have no plan. No clue what you are up against. It's like we are the Ewoks in this battle. Not exactly Jedi material," he said with a weak smile. He hoped his Star Wars joke would lighten the mood.

"But I need to act. I mean ... clearly something is happening," retorted Kris.

Niko stared at his chicken patty, then over at Kris's untouched patty. "Are you going to eat that?" he asked.

"You can have it Niko. After class let's just go to the river and see what ideas we have," suggested Kris.

"Bonus!" exclaimed Niko as he reached for Kris's patty. "I guess it's the only thing we can do." Niko seemed to resign himself to the fact that they were not yet equipped to understand how to proceed.

CHAPTER TWENTY

SCHOOL WAS OUT before they knew it. The day, and its corresponding dread, moved faster than either Kris or Niko could have imagined. As they left the building, the news trucks made another appearance. Clearly, the missing girl was still missing.

Police cars circled the area, as did other cars with volunteers looking for Daria. Kris saw Daria's teacher talking to the police. A look of pain and tears apparent even from a distance.

The other kids were quiet. Everyone looked scared as the parents descended upon the school in droves. It looked like no one was willing to let their child walk home.

Suddenly Kris heard his mom "Kris, you must have heard about that little girl. Parents are picking up because no one knows if the neighborhood is safe. Niko, I told your mom I would get you too."

Kris and Niko gave each other a look. "Thanks mom. Just remember … me and Niko look out for each other. Anyone messing with either of us is messing with both of us," said Kris.

"Double trouble with a side of spinach pie," his mom joked. Their family was Greek. The parents always seemed to lighten the mood with a Greek joke, or Greek food reference, whenever it fit.

"Wait auntie. Did you make spinach pie for dinner tonight?" Niko said, completely serious.

Kris and his mom couldn't help but laugh. Niko's stomach was always on overdrive for Greek food, despite the situation. After the moment of levity, Kris's mom asked "did you guys know the little girl?"

"Well, yeah. I am betting she will turn up real soon mom. She has some special needs. We both used to hang out with her in the after school program," said Kris.

"Oh honey," his mom said, suddenly teary. "You both must be so worried for her."

Niko and Kris were having difficulty looking worried given what they knew was happening. Despite this, the boys knew they should say something. "Uh, it's unbelievable," said Niko softly. "But more unbelievable your mom was only kidding about the spinach pie," he whispered to Kris.

"Yeah mom. Just a few weeks ago everything in this town was so easy, so safe. Now it's hard to imagine that any of this is happening," said Kris.

"Life is crazy boys. Just when you think things appear one way, they can change drastically. The world is unpredictable, and not always in good ways. I really sympathize with Daria's mom. Kris when you were missing … I thought I would go insane looking for you," said Kris's mom seriously.

Kris's mom grew teary again. She looked at her son. She wrapped her arm around his shoulder. As Kris felt the touch from his mother, he was jolted by an image of his mom driving around the neighborhood. She was crying, calling out his name, and praying to God for his safe return. Kris realized he could see and feel her emotions. His gift was growing stronger and stronger.

"We could help look for Daria," said Kris.

"Yeah. We could join the search party," said Niko.

"Do you guys have ideas on where to look?" said his mom.

"We know Daria likes, uh … water. So maybe that's a start," said Niko. Kris shot Niko a look, unsure of whether this was a good idea or not.

"Do you think she would go in a neighbor's pool or something like that?" asked Kris's mom. Clearly, she was trying to piece together the broad clue Niko threw out.

"Yeah mom. She could just be lost and swimming. The weather is still warm. You know how some kids just love water so much that they lose all track of time and stuff?" said Kris.

"When we get home, let's make a plan to cover the neighborhood pools in our area. Great idea guys. We will do everything we can to help," said Kris's mom.

When the three got home they printed a simple street map from their computer. They wanted to ensure that they could move through the neighborhood in a systematic and efficient manner. After a quick bathroom run, Kris's mom packed snacks and water bottles in a backpack. The three headed outside to begin the search.

"OK guys, let's just go door to door. Of course, if we know a neighbor does not have a pool we can skip the house. If we are unsure let's ring the bell. I want you both to stay close and move together. I will take the odd side of the street. You guys will work across from me on the even side. After we check a house, let's meet on the sidewalk and go forward together. Got it?" said Kris's mom.

"Roger that mom," said Kris quickly. He and Niko headed to the first house. They knew it was occupied by an elderly couple who indeed had a small, shallow pool in their yard.

When they were alone, Kris finally spoke. "Niko, this is disastrous. You and your water idea!"

"I had to say something, " said Niko defensively. "This town is in crisis. It's not like our parents are about to let us run off and play."

"Ah! We need to think of a way to get to the river Niko! Something terrible is happening. I mean ... must be happening," said Kris emphatically.

"Well, I cannot fathom how we are going to break free Kris. This is not exactly the ideal time to go missing."

Kris and Niko knocked on the door of the house they stood in front of. Ms. Tuner, a sweet little old lady, poked her head out. Just as Kris started to explain why they were there, Ms. Turner said "Oh, it's all over the news channel my dears. Check my backyard. Of course, you are welcome to look here as long as you want."

Kris and Niko rounded the house. They went into the backyard, knowing that Daria would not be there given the simple fact that she was in the river. Kris, his mom, and his cousin moved from house to house for blocks with the same result. Suddenly they came upon Albie's street.

Kris and Niko both felt a chill at the exact time they saw Albie's house. Neither of them factored Albie into the search equation, even though they both felt Albie must hold key information. Kris's mom went to the house across the street. Kris and Niko knocked on Albie's door.

They were not surprised to see the blonde woman with the sparkly rings answer in a cheery 'hello'.

"Uh, hi. We are trying to find our friend Daria. She has been missing and we know she loves water. We were wondering if you had a pool because she might be in it," started Niko.

"Oh, of course," said Albie's mom with a sincere look on her face. "You boys are incredible, really. I remember you from the time I picked Albie up from extended day. You guys are so caring. We actually do have a pool. I have not been in the backyard all day! Come on through the house and I will let you out to the patio. You are welcome to look around as long as you like," said Albie's mom.

Suddenly the boys heard a grunting sound and a small thud. Before they knew it, Albie was walking right toward them with what looked like a cassette player in his hand.

Kris and Niko froze into place. Albie's steel eyes looked at them carefully.

"You remember Albie of course," said his mother.

"Hi Albie," said Kris robotically.

"Yeah. Hi," added Niko.

Albie just stood in the hallway motionless. It was as if he knew something was happening that should not.

"Well boys, maybe Albie can help you look around. He loves the outdoors. Our yard is large and well fenced, so he can walk around with you," said Albie's mom.

Niko swallowed so hard he thought the whole room heard it. Kris just shook his head as the blonde lady took Albie's hand and started walking to what looked like a kitchen area. Before they knew it, Albie's mom opened a sliding door. She ushered all three kids onto the patio.

"Anyone want cookies?" she asked cheerily.

"No thanks. I just had some snack," said Kris as Niko shot him a *come on, let's eat* look.

"Well, Albie loves cookies. I will fix a plate and if you change your mind you can eat," said Albie's mom.

"Sounds great," said Niko with a smile.

The blonde lady went back into the house as Kris and Niko started to walk around the yard. Albie trailed them suspiciously. He was staring hard at Niko.

"What's his problem?" said Niko in a whisper.

"He knows you want his cookies Niko," Kris said as he slapped Niko's shoulder. "But seriously, think! he knows everything. Maybe he knew we were watching."

Suddenly Albie rocketed towards Kris. He stood right in front of him. Kris could feel his breath on his face, and sense the heat from his body. Out of instinct Niko stepped up ready to intervene.

Albie raised his large hand in slow motion, ready to grab Kris's neck. With a lightning quick response Niko grabbed Albie's wrist. A burst of light appeared in the sky and Kris heard Niko yell sharply. Then something blinded Kris, and in an instant Niko and Albie vanished.

Kris looked around frantically, fear shaking him to the core. He spun around a few times as sweat formed on his forehead. They were gone. Within seconds he knew what needed to be done. He knew that Albie meant to touch him. Niko's interference was an unexpected mistake. Kris hopped the fence and ran out of the yard as fast as he could, heading straight for the river.

As Kris ran his blood pounded in his ears. He quickly calculated the situation. He concluded that Daria and Albie had Niko, and that they knew everything about that night at the river. He reasoned that Niko was likely being held by them to bait him.

Blue warned him about the war. Now the aliens actually declared war on a human. Kris fought back tears as he thought of his cousin. He could see the river come into view. In a superhuman, half amphibian way he jumped through the air and dove straight into the water. Once submerged, Kris screamed as loud as he could. He let the swampy water fill his lungs. He grabbed a branch at the bottom of the river and held on tight.

The familiar pain across his neck came fast as Kris felt himself transform to a water breather. Kris's eyes opened wide as he scanned the water. His skin camouflaged perfectly with the river's bottom. It was eerily quiet for a few seconds as he began to swim. Kris quickly moved in the direction of the cave. Suddenly he froze himself into place as he noticed a dead frog float past him. Gripped with anger, he spun himself around then let out a mighty croak. He could sense that an enemy was near. His instinct was to use one of his calls.

Kris shot through the water with new force. He could see the cave ahead of him. Flanking the entrance was an army of wounded frogs, some already floating lifelessly in the water. Kris neared one of the frogs. He reached to it and gripped its small webbed foreleg. In a painful flash a series of war images filled his mind. He could see silver flashes of light cutting through the river. He watched underwater explosions, and cries of pain. He could see an army of aliens disguised as kids. One of them, Daria, advanced on the cave. He could see another alien holding Blue in a tight grip, laughing.

Kris entered the cave. He called out to Blue. There was no answer, only an unnatural silence. The emptiness began to panic Kris as he called out to Blue again.

Suddenly Kris could see something coming towards him from the corner of his eye. He spun quickly to see that the wounded, three-legged frog slowly paddling towards him was actually Blue.

"Human, we are truly at war," Blue said weakly.

"Blue, I saw. I know. They took my cousin, my best friend Niko," said Kris shakily.

Blue looked at Kris, surprised. "Human, this is a new tactic. A more psychological one."

"Blue where are they?" Kris said in an exasperated tone.

"Here in the river, human. They set up a base further north. It is without question that they took the other human there. They have been observing human emotion for years. Quickly learning the value of ransom."

"Is he OK?" asked Kris in a frightened voice.

"He should be. He is no use to them unless he is alive," said Blue.

"I need to find them. To get Niko. To stop them," said Kris.

"And we will. Our army is down, but the creatures of the river have no allegiance to the aliens so we will have more help," said Blue.

Suddenly a loud crack echoed through the cave. "What was that?" screamed Kris.

"The aliens are destroying the river. They are building an underwater base so they can hide. Clever, so clever they are human. After they take over the river, they will make attacks on land and then disappear back to the water. No one will even think to search for them under the surface. They have it all planned out. If anyone spies one of them coming into the woods, it will only look like a lost, innocent child. One that cannot be held accountable for wandering off," said Blue as he spun weakly by Kris's nose.

"If we can win back the kids, I mean their physical forms, then the aliens will not be able to disguise themselves. I saw how the alien entered one kid. I watched a kid at the river. Watched an alien beam right into him. If they can beam in, then they can definitely beam out," said Kris with an air of confidence.

"The human form is like a jacket for them. A Halloween costume. They are not dominant enough to show themselves. They need an army to do that! They are building that army," said Blue sadly.

Just as Kris was about to respond, a large boxer turtle entered the cave. His size was immense. He must have measured at least two feet across his back. His shell was cracked and it looked charred. The shell appeared as if it were struck by lightning.

"Milan," said Blue calmly.

"The hunters have retreated for some reason. The blasting and construction for the take-over is still going. I am sure you heard the blasts," said Milan.

Kris stared at the turtle and quickly asked "have you heard anything on the aliens taking a human with them?"

The turtle looked at Kris with a serious, calm expression. "No," he firmly replied.

"Do you know where the aliens would hide a human?" Kris asked rapidly.

"Yes. They would need to use an area of the river that has a dry peak. An area deep within the rock. There are several like this. Hidden pockets with tunnels that lead to land. Tunnels that bring air to the spaces. But the tunnels are narrow, impossible for a human to fit into. The only way in them is through water," said the turtle in the same stern tone.

"You have to show me Milan," said Kris seriously.

"We will need reinforcements. And what of your translator human?" said Milan.

"Uh, well … I still have no idea who or what my translator is," said Kris in an exasperated tone.

Milan and Blue looked at each other. They were surprised that Kris had no idea. "Well, you possess a power from it. Only one that you and your translator share. We do not know what the power is," said Milan.

"I cannot waste time figuring it out. There is no time to lose," said Kris.

"Agreed," said Blue.

"Let's move out. Before the night falls," said Milan.

CHAPTER TWENTY-ONE

BLUE HOPPED ATOP Milan's shell. The giant turtle strode ahead swiftly. Kris glided through the water with ease, his webbed hands slicing through the river water. Blue let out a series of croaks and clicks. Before they knew it the three were surrounded by what looked like one hundred turtles. The turtles were all large. They had thick webbed legs, and sharp menacing claws. They looked fearless. They were well protected by their thick broad shells.

"We will conduct a search," started Blue. "The human warrior is being baited. The aliens have taken another human in hopes to draw him in. I suspect it's a trap of some kind. We need to act fast. Our goal is to recover the other human, remove him from the river to a safe location, and destroy as many hunters as possible."

"Agreed," the turtle army said in unison.

"Each of you should be accompanied by a frog that fires poisons. We have learned that our poisons can damage the vision of the enemy, in the way of burning," said Blue.

"Aim for the eyes," added Milan.

From the bottom of the river rose a mass of tiny frogs. They were hiding in the mud, waiting to be summoned. "Onwards," said Blue.

Blue's command was followed by clicks, croaks, and the sound of turtle claws thrashing in the water. Kris swam alongside the mass of turtles and frogs. They came to a point in the river where several rocky projections divided the trail. Without a word, the mass of turtles and frogs split into groups of twenty.

Kris knew he needed to choose a group, so he swam to and joined the group on the left. The warriors stealthily glided into a narrow, dark cave. Even with his incredible vision, it was difficult for Kris to see more than three feet ahead.

Kris was the largest warrior with the group. He worked hard to avoid cutting himself on the black rock that formed the entrance to the underwater tunnel. Despite his agile moves, one of his feet scraped along the wall as he progressed. As his foot rubbed against the wall, a burst of pain shot through Kris.

Kris closed his eyes and could see a vision of the enemy. He could see this as clearly as he saw images when he touched the frogs. It was clear that the large human bodies of the enemies scraped those exact walls, just as he was scraping them now. He winced as a vision of Daria, and some other children he had never seen before, showed them swimming through the narrow passage. Then he saw a horrifying image. He saw one of the kids hiding out in the muddy bottom of the unfamiliar cave. Hiding and waiting.

Kris rocketed over to Blue and touched one of his remaining legs. In a flash the image was translated to Blue … but it came too late. It was a trap! Up from the mud rose a sea of human hands, ready to destroy.

Kris felt something grab his legs. Superhuman strength held him firmly into place as he tried to kick. Around him the turtle army tried to claw at the hands that held their shells. The tiny frogs shot their poison. The frogs inflicted small wounds as they shot poison at the eyes of the enemy. Kris felt himself growing warmer and warmer. Something was happening.

Kris could feel his skin growing slimy. He was secreting something that loosened the enemies grip. Kris's hands reached down to locate the enemy. He found the ears of his captor and held them firmly. An image of Niko opened in his mind. He could see Niko, freezing and cold. He was crying on a rock as a menacing alien approached.

Kris's body temperature rose higher. He could feel the ears of the alien melting in his fingers. He reached across the alien's face. He put his hands to the alien's eyes. His poisonous touch caused an immediate release.

Kris dove ahead in the direction of a turtle gripped by four hands. The hands held a shiny silver rod that was slicing the turtle's shell as if it were butter. Kris gripped two of the hands. He watched as the poison burned the enemy. Flashes of information competed with his concentration. Images of Niko gasping for air came to him, maddening him further.

Kris let out a deafening croak. His anger was all consuming. More hands attempted to grip him. The amount of poison he was producing left a slimy covering on his skin. The slimy coating prevented the aliens from capturing him.

Kris spun around as he searched for Blue. He watched as a hand swiftly moved through the air. It yanked Blue down by one of his tiny legs. Furious, Kris rocketed down in the direction of the hand. He spied a captured and unconscious Blue. Kris reached for the wrist of the enemy, and melted the flesh to bone.

As the alien's hand opened, Blue floated out. His eyes were open and unblinking. Kris cradled Blue in his palm as he fought back tears. Flashes of the attack on Blue tried to make their way into Kris's mind, but the signals coming from Blue were weak.

Kris sensed that one of Blue's remaining forelegs was broken. He watched it wave slowly back and forth in response to the water. Kris was about to swim ahead when he felt a heavy object blanket his shoulders and head. He struggled to move away from it, but its weight was like lead. Kris was caught in a net.

CHAPTER TWENTY-TWO

THE ENEMY WAS tricky. They learned quickly that Kris could not be held by touch. His ability to poison was far too strong. But he could be held by something else. He felt the net dragging him further into the tunnel.

The semi-darkness grew to pitch black. His amphibian eyes, although able to see some of his surroundings, lost their total clarity. Kris held Blue in his palm as they moved on. The fight between aliens, turtles, and frogs raged on as he was pulled out of sight.

Kris felt a moment of helplessness engulf him as he looked at Blue. He did not struggle for the moment. Instead he tried to think of a plan. He realized he was alone. Although he had the power to absorb images, Blue was too injured to transmit any. Kris had no idea what lay ahead.

Kris jerked his head forward as he heard a screech. It sounded like a large underwater gate was opening in the distance. Kris attempted to make out the source of the noise, but could not decipher it.

The tunnel began to grow a bit lighter. Kris could tell that it also grew wider. The net moved forward. Then it seemed to be rising upwards and out of the water. Kris instinctively shifted to the bottom of the net. He needed to breathe water and he knew it.

As he flattened his body at the base of the net, he gazed upwards to see that he was coming face to face with Albie. But the Albie before him was filled with cold intent. The Albie before him did not have a blank stare. He had an expression of dominance and power. And this Albie could speak.

"Human, I am a general in this war. One of the finest leaders in the outer realm. By now you know that off-Earth beings are destined to take back your planet. It has been planned this way since the end of the dinosaurs. We cannot, and will not, be stopped. I demand to know who you have told about the war," the alien Albie boomed.

Kris stared around him, noticing how quiet the space was. The alien Albie was standing on land. He was at the highest point in the cave. Outside light shone in from a narrow air tunnel above.

The alien Albie was alone. Prior to Kris's capture, he directed his warriors to other areas of the river. He stayed back to deal with Kris. Undoubtedly, the enemy was trying to figure out what defenses the human may have.

"I have told our mightiest warriors," bluffed Kris. "They will be coming. Your disguises won't fool people any longer. We know all about you!" Kris threatened.

The alien Albie let out a laugh. "Really human? For all your secret spying on us at the place called school, it's unlikely that you spread the word to so many. Confess the truth. You do not have many contacts, but we would be happy to capture them all if you would prefer that."

Suddenly Kris felt the net move upward. He felt his head break the surface of the water. He gasped, flailing with Blue in his palm. The net was again lowered. The enemy stared at Kris as he watched him suck in water. "We know you need to breathe water now human. We can destroy you with the simplest of weapons ... air," said the alien Albie with a sickening smile on his face.

"I will trade information with you," yelled Kris, "once you release Niko."

"So we thought," said the alien Albie.

"I want to know where Niko is," said Kris.

"Turn and see," said the alien Albie as he pointed a pruned finger to his right side.

Kris turned his head to see Niko. He was suspended vertically in some strange type of air tube. The tube was on the land, in a dark corner of the cave. Niko did not move. He looked stunned. He was motionless.

"What did you do to Niko!" Kris screamed, a poisonous cloud emerging from his skin.

"We prepared him for the greatest gift, being a disguise for our army," said the enemy with another terrible smile. "I may just wear his skin next."

Kris was horrified. "I did not tell anyone. Just Niko, that's all," he said quickly.

The alien Albie stared at Kris in disbelief. Kris felt the net being raised. His head was again out of water. He was being dragged onto the land, to the middle of the cave. At the cave's center was a moonlit space. The area was illuminated by a narrow tunnel that led to the top of the earth. Kris gasped uncontrollably. He watched the enemy continuing to pull the net from the water. Kris tried to reach his free hand out of the net to grip his enemies' leg, but the need for water weakened his abilities.

"Human, we will soon do to you what we did to the dinosaurs. We will take the planet you so greatly restored. Then we will use your human forms as we choose," said the alien Albie.

Kris was now at the center of the cave's air pocket. The water was at least ten feet away. Kris was trapped, helpless, and losing time. He wondered how long he could hold on. He felt his body grow motionless as he rolled onto his back.

Kris stared at his adversary. He was making his way to the tube Niko was in. Kris felt himself weaken further. He gasped for water. His gaze shifted to the small moonlit opening that led to the now dark, night sky. As he looked towards the sky he felt his mind play tricks on him. He thought he saw the most beautiful star in the world. His mind suddenly flashed back to his childhood. He thought of his mom. He thought of being a little boy, looking at the stars, singing 'twinkle, twinkle'.

And in that instant his mind remembered. Kris recalled everything. As a child he once wished on a star. He wished he could swim like a fish. That wish came true. He proved that wish to his family on that fateful vacation, but his skill at transforming from a human to a water breather was only just evolving. Kris got lost in an underwater adventure. He found his way out only months later.

More of that childhood memory flooded his mind. Kris recalled wanting to swim to the surface to find his mom, but getting distracted by the beautiful colors, creatures, and spaces of the underwater world. He got lost for months. Lost until he made a wish. Kris's mom always told him to wish on the brightest star. She told him his wishes would come true. And that was how Kris found his way home. He made a wish to see his mother again. The second he did this, he woke up in a hospital.

The doctors called it a coma, but Kris knew better. He was just on an adventure, one he wished for. He tried to tell his mother all about it. She just smiled and told him he had an incredible dream while his body was resting. Kris was very young at the time, and quickly forgot about the whole experience. His family never discussed it again. Everyone just seemed to move on and forget. In another instant Kris knew exactly what to do. He closed his eyes and whispered "I wish I could breathe air."

And just like that … he was a land breather. Kris realized that the star, who had always been there when he transformed, was his translator. Kris sprung up to his feet. He felt a power in his hands unlike anything he knew. His fingers softly glowed as beautifully as a star in the night. Kris sliced through the net with one hand. He gently placed Blue in a shallow area of water in a corner of the cave.

Kris made his way towards the alien Albie. The space creature had its back towards Kris. It was attending to something on Niko's tube. The enemy was too distracted to notice that Kris escaped. As Kris got closer, the sound of his footsteps was detectable. The enemy spun around to see what was behind him. Kris was already on top of the alien by the time he figured out that Kris escaped the net.

As the two rolled on the ground, the alien Albie pulled a thin, silver weapon from his pinky finger. The enemy sprung forward, and regained his footing. He moved the silver stick like a sword as he watched Kris stand up.

"Give it up human. You are weak," said the alien Albie.

Kris felt a flood of emotion as he prepared to advance on the enemy again. Kris jumped high in the air and landed on the alien. The two crashed back to the ground and wrestled, as Kris endured cuts with the silver weapon. The poison remaining on Kris's skin wounded the enemy a little, but it did not stop him.

Suddenly Kris heard a voice in his head "human, you are the one that can win this war." It was Blue's voice. The alien Albie could somehow sense what Kris was hearing, as if their wrestling lock was another conduit for images and sounds. The alien rolled his human body away from Kris. He made his way to the shallow pool that contained Blue. He dipped his hand in the water and scooped out Blue.

"All because of you!" he bellowed to the small frog. The alien Albie then tore Blue in half. He threw his small remains in the water, where they sank quietly to the bottom of the mud.

Kris felt a new outrage. He sprung into the air and landed on the alien Albie again. His fingers were pulsing, glowing. A superhuman heat was now mounting from his skin. Kris held the enemy's arms. Thin rays of light jutted from his fingers, disabling the enemy instantly. His adversary began to go limp in the process. Kris reached for the alien Albie's throat and let the magical light cut through the enemy. His adversary fell unconscious on the ground. Kris knew instinctively that the alien was dead.

Kris next sprung over to the air tube that held Niko. He smashed his fist through it with a loud bang. He pulled Niko, entirely limp, from the opening he made. He hoisted Niko over his shoulder.

And as if it was the most natural thing in the world, Kris moved to the highest point in the cave. He stood under the air tunnel. He raised his hand to the night sky. A burst of light flew from his fingers. It blasted the rock, widening the air tunnel that led to land. All Kris had to do was spring up, an easy feat for a boy who was half frog. He bent his knees as he secured Niko over his shoulder and jumped with all his might. Before he knew it, he was standing on land, under the light of the magical star.

Kris gently placed Niko on the soft grass as he tried to rouse him "Niko, come on cousin. It's me Kris. I have you now. It's all going to be OK," he said as tears formed in his eyes. He had never seen Niko helpless before. Never seen him need anything. The weight of this penetrated Kris as he stared at Niko.

Niko lay motionless. He was cold, but Kris could see a quick rise in his chest. He was breathing. "How do I fix this?" he said to himself as he reached down and hugged his best friend. "How do I get you back?"

Kris held Niko and cried in the starlight. Flashbacks of all their good times played in his mind, which deepened his pain. And as natural as could be, he whispered "Niko, I wish I could turn you back to normal."

Kris was crying too hard to see the glow from the sky, or even the glow from his body. But suddenly he heard a voice in his ear. "Kris, it's about time," said Niko slowly.

Kris hugged Niko as tightly as he could. He knew it was OK. Niko was back.

"Did we win?" asked Niko, as he scanned the land for a clue.

"For now, cousin," said Kris pensively. "We lost Blue, but the alien Albie is gone. He was leading the invasion. I wish you could have seen me in action," said Kris.

And before he realized what he said, the images of the battle scene coursed through Niko. Their touching shoulders served as a conduit. Niko stared at Kris in amazement.

"I am sorry about Blue. He was so brave. Do you think I have powers too, cousin?" asked Niko.

Kris had no idea whether or not Niko had powers. He was still discovering his own powers, and trying to come to grips with the fact that the world was more than just Earth. All Kris knew for sure was that if you truly believed, anything was possible. It was his beliefs, his dreams, and his wishes that made him who he was … even if he was only remembering it just now.

Kris pulled Niko to his feet and the two began to walk home.

Katina Lawdis is an American science fiction writer. She has been publishing stories since 2009. Known mainly for her children's books, Katina has authored eight books for elementary school audiences.

These books include the trilogy: *Twinkle the Star: The Ocean Adventure*, *Twinkle the Star: The Dinosaur Adventure*, *Twinkle the Star: Castle Island*. *The Frogs Warning* is intended for young adult to older audiences, and contains surprise connections to the *Twinkle the Star* series. Children who grew up with the *Twinkle the Star* trilogy can grow into *The Frogs Warning*, making these connected stories enjoyable for generations.

In 2022, Katina made the cover and character art from *The Frogs Warning* available digitally as NFTs. Visit https://opensea.io/collection/klawdis to view and bid on these one of a kind NFTs.

Additionally, *Imagination with a Scoop of Monsters*, *The Koi Who Cried Wolf*, *The Three Hares*, *Lions in my Tummy ~ A Tale of Animal Cookies Gone Wild*, and *The Boy Who Cried Wolf Fish* are among her other childrens works.

Katina has also published one book of poetry called *Wisdom of the Heart: A Valentine Book*.